Peter's day is going from bad to worse. First he loses his job, then he finds out his apartment flooded. He has nothing left but his sister, and she lives in another city.

Sean doesn't know what to expect when he agrees to give his best friend's brother a job and a place to stay, but he feels sorry for the guy, especially when Peter calls him because his car broke down on his way to town.

Peter's luck is rotten, or at least, it is until he meets Sean. Because Sean is his mate, and Peter is home with him.

He doesn't feel that way, though. Peter wants to be with Sean, but he's afraid. He can't allow himself to depend on anyone, not even his mate. He has to show himself and the world that he can stand on his own two feet, but when it could mean losing Sean, he'll have to make a decision.

Will he make the right one?

Leap of Faith
Copyright © 2020 Catherine Lievens
ISBN: 978-1-4874-3086-3
Cover art by Angela Waters

Published by eXtasy Books Inc or
Devine Destinies, an imprint of eXtasy Books Inc

Look for us online at:
www.eXtasybooks.com or www.devinedestinies.com

Leap of Faith
Seven Brothers 3

By

Catherine Lievens

CHAPTER ONE

Peter didn't love being an accountant. He didn't think *anyone* loved being an accountant. He wasn't sure why he'd chosen this job except for the fact that he was good at math and he had a degree, but he had, which was why he wasn't exactly happy when the boss called him to his office. When that happened, it meant something bad was going on, and Peter tried to remember if he'd done anything. He didn't think so, but what did he know? He wasn't the boss, and he didn't care about the same things Rupert did.

He stared at the office door, wondering what was going on in there. He hadn't been the only one called in, and from the faces of the people who left, he knew that whatever it was, *was* bad.

He tapped his fingertips onto his knee. He wanted to run away, but he couldn't. He couldn't hide under his blankets so the monster wouldn't find him. He couldn't avoid this, couldn't avoid being an adult and having to face what being an adult meant.

The door flew open, and a woman came out. He'd seen her around the office, but they didn't work together. Still, he wanted to comfort her when he saw that her eyes were full of tears. Instead, he stayed right where he was, and she straightened. She nodded at herself, not even looking at Peter, and strode away from the boss's office with purpose.

Peter swallowed. He was the only one left, so he knew it was his turn now.

He had a pretty good idea of what was happening, but he

told himself not to overthink it. Maybe it was nothing. Maybe his boss only wanted to talk about clients.

Maybe he was about to get fired.

He got to his feet, rubbed his trembling hands onto his thighs, and headed for the door since it was still open. When he peeked in, he knew he was right. Rupert was behind his desk, looking pale, rubbing his face as if he wasn't enjoying what was happening. He probably wasn't, either. The man wasn't evil, and while he wasn't exactly Peter's friend, they'd been friendly the few times they'd talked. He and Peter always said hello when they saw each other in the hallways, and whatever the reason he had to fire people, it had to be serious. Peter couldn't imagine it was easy.

But then, his own life would be far from easy as soon as he got out the door.

Rupert looked up and grimaced at the sight of Peter peeking in. "Peter. Come in."

Peter wanted to shake his head and move away from the door, but instead he stepped into the office and closed the door behind him. Then he hovered there, wondering *what now*.

Rupert waved at the chairs on the other side of his desk. "Sit down."

Peter didn't say anything. He obeyed, his heart racing in his chest.

Okay, so he didn't love being an accountant, but he was good at it. Besides, if he wasn't an accountant, it meant he didn't have a job, and that was a problem. He had to pay rent and utilities. He had to put some money away for rainy days.

The problem was that this seemed to have become a rainy day, and he didn't have enough savings.

"I'm sorry," Rupert said. "I'm not happy to do this, but the business is closing. All of you will have to find new jobs."

Peter swallowed. He'd expected it, and he didn't want to

snap. Rupert had been an okay boss, and he'd given Peter a chance right after Peter had graduated. "Can I ask what's happening?"

Rupert looked away from Peter. "I'm moving to Florida. My wife, you know? She doesn't like it here. She wanted to live in a warmer climate, and that means closing the business and starting a new one."

Peter hadn't expected that. He'd thought the business was failing, maybe. He hadn't even thought twice about Rupert's wife. "So you're just kicking all of us out?"

"I'm not kicking you out, no. I'll do everything by the book. But the business is closing, Peter, which means you have to find a new job. I've been letting people go all morning, and most of them haven't taken it well. I'm hoping you won't yell at me."

The attempt at humor didn't touch Peter. He'd been so busy that he hadn't even realized that people were being let go. He should have. It certainly explained why the office seemed to be so empty at this time of day. It shouldn't have been, but if people left the building as soon as they talked to Rupert, it made sense.

Peter swallowed. His mouth tasted like metal, and he wasn't sure why. "All right. I'll go, then."

Rupert looked relieved. Peter didn't know what had happened before he got here, but he could easily imagine. Not all the people who worked here were as meek as he was.

"Thanks for not making this harder than it is," Rupert commented.

Peter almost snorted. What did Rupert know about *hard*? Even though he was closing his business, he would start a new one in Florida. He wouldn't have to think about how he was going to pay rent or how he would buy food. Hell, even if he never opened another business, he didn't have to worry about any of that. He was rich. His father was rich. Peter never understood why he had opened this office, and he still didn't. He also didn't care.

He got to his feet. He hoped he would manage to get to the door without falling on his face, even though his legs felt like jelly. Now that he knew what was going on, his thoughts were focused on the new problems he would have to deal with.

Finding a new job would be hell. He could do it, though. He would have to.

"Thank you," Rupert said again. "You can send anyone who's still out there inside."

Peter nodded, but he did nothing of the sort. There was another man in the waiting area when he left the office, but just like the woman before him had done, he limited himself to leaving the door open and headed to his desk.

Luckily for him, he didn't have a lot of things to pack, so he was out of the building only twenty minutes later. He took a deep breath, glancing at the sky. It was about to rain, which would be the perfect end to this day, wouldn't it?

Peter was wrong. The perfect—perfectly horrible—end to the day was what he found when he got home.

"What's going on?" he asked his landlord when he found the man standing in front of the building, looking up at it.

A lot of the other people who lived in the building were also there, some talking, a few crying. Peter's stomach churned, and he wondered if he had an antiacid left in his messenger bag.

Alfred jerked and took a step back. "Peter."

"Is something happening, or can I go home?" Peter asked, even though the answer was obvious. There were firefighters everywhere he looked, and if the situation hadn't been dire, he might have done a bit of people-watching.

Alfred rubbed the back of his neck. "Well, see, there was a problem. Your apartment and several others are flooded."

Peter blinked, sure he'd misheard that. "Flooded?"

"A pipe ruptured. They're full of water. I'm sorry, Peter. I'm not allowed in, and I don't think the firefighters will allow you, either. There's water everywhere, and they're pumping the water out and making sure the structure is sound."

Peter looked at the building. "I have to grab my things, though." He didn't know where he would go, but he would find a place. He had to.

"You can try talking to the firefighters, but I doubt they'll allow you in. I'm *really* sorry. It's going to be a while before I manage to get it fixed."

"Are you telling me that I have to find a new apartment?"

"It would be for the best. Since I have to fix it, I'm thinking about selling once it's done, although of course, the new owners might want to keep you on."

Peter looked at the ground to keep from crying. What was he supposed to do now?

He looked back up, thought about needing to find a new job, a new apartment, new everything, and took his phone out.

He called his sister.

Sean's phone rang while he was checking the day's work. He paused in the middle of the newly renovated living room he was in and took his phone out of his pocket. Just like always when he saw that Emily was calling him, he grinned.

He and Emily had been best friends for what felt like forever, and he would always answer when she called.

Mac was painting the finishing touches around the light switch. Sean patted him on the back and gestured he was heading outside. Mac nodded and went back to work, obviously wanting to finish this by the end of the day.

"Rat!" he said as he answered.

He could hear the scowl in Emily's voice. "I already told

you not to call me that. I'm not a rat."

"All right, all right. I'm sorry. Do you need anything? Because if you don't, I'll have to call you back. I'm about to head home and shower before heading over to my parents' house. I can call you back once I feel more human."

"Really? Because you're *not* human."

"Neither are you." Although she wasn't a rat shifter, he liked to tease her. She was a hedgehog, which was why they'd become friends in college. They'd been the only shifters around, and it had been weird after growing up with six brothers. Emily, too, had been lonely, and now she and Sean were their own little chosen family. It was more important to her since she didn't talk to her parents anymore, but Sean loved it, too, and he loved her.

"What can I do for you?" he asked, more serious. There had to be a reason she was calling now.

Emily sighed. "I need help."

Sean frowned. He didn't like the sound of her voice. "Wait a second. I'm going outside so we can talk."

"There's nothing to talk about. Just say you'll help me."

"You know I will. Do I have to kill someone?"

Emily barked out a laugh, and it was nice to hear it. It meant that whatever it was wasn't as bad as Sean had expected—hopefully.

He stepped out of the house. He would have to go back in to say goodbye to the owners and send the team home, but in the meantime, he and Emily could talk. "Come on. Tell me what's going on."

Sean hated the fact that they lived in different cities now. It made sense for Emily's work, and for his. He didn't work with his father anymore, but he had his own construction company, and he'd opened it in his hometown. Emily, on the other hand, lived in a big city.

"It's my brother. I'm sorry, but he just called me, and he

was panicking. On the same day, he lost his job and his apartment, and from the sound of it, everything he owns."

Sean grimaced. He'd never met Peter, but he'd heard a lot about him through Emily. "Just tell me what you need me to do."

"Thank you. I knew you'd help."

"Anything for you." And Sean wasn't kidding.

"He needs a new job, obviously. He also needs a place to stay, though. His apartment flooded, and he only has the clothes on his back. He doesn't even know if he'll be allowed back inside to see if anything survived."

"He doesn't live around here, does he?"

"No. He lives in Boston. He can get to you soon, though. If you give him a job, he'll be eager to start."

No doubt because he needed it. If what Emily was saying was true, Peter would have to rebuy everything he owned. That meant he needed money, and to earn it, he would have to work.

"I can give him a job, no problem." Sean paused and frowned. "Remind me what job he does?"

"I love you," Emily said instead.

"I love you too. Now tell me."

"He's an accountant. Apparently, the business where he's working is closing. Something about the owner moving to Florida? I don't know. He was pretty out of it when he called me. He was standing in front of his building, and there was a lot of noise. He was kind of freaking out."

"Understandable. Okay. Tell him he can work with me. No problem. I can't promise him that he'll do the accounting, though." Because Peter ready had an accountant, and he didn't think there was a place for Peter in his business, not as an accountant. As long as Peter didn't mind doing other things, though, it wouldn't be a problem.

"I'll tell him. And I'll make sure to tell him he won't be able to play with numbers for you. He just needs something to tide him over until he finds another job."

"I know it's not ideal, but this, I can offer him." Sean hesitated. This was Emily's brother, and even though they'd never met, it made him family. "I also have a guest room for him if he's okay with that. It can be only in the beginning, until he earns enough money to get his own place."

"Oh, thank God. I was afraid to ask. Thank you, Sean. I don't know what I would have done without you."

"You probably would have died the first year of college," Sean teased her.

"That, or I would have dropped out. I don't know, and honestly, I don't want to think about it. Just—thank you."

"You don't have to keep thanking me. You're family."

"But you never met Peter. Maybe you'll hate him." She hesitated. "He's gay, you know?"

That made Sean smile. "So? I'm not going to ask him to pay rent in any way, monetary or otherwise." He didn't need the money, while Peter could use a break.

Emily huffed. "That's not what I meant."

"I know."

"I just wanted to be sure you remembered and that it wasn't a surprise or anything."

Sean cleared his throat. "Give him my phone number. Tell him to call me for anything. I'll get the guest room ready for when he arrives, and I can buy some stuff if he needs me to, like toiletries or whatnot."

"I'll call him. Thank you, Sean."

"*Stop* thanking me. It's what I do for family." Although Emily had never fully understood that.

They hung up, and Peter looked up at the sky. He didn't know what he'd gotten himself into. He'd never met Peter, since he'd dropped out of college to work with his dad, and Peter was a few years younger than he and Emily. Sean had come back home after leaving college while Emily had stuck around, and the few times he'd visited, Peter had been busy with his own things.

But Peter was Emily's brother. He needed help, and Sean was more than happy to help him out in any way he could. He might not know Peter, but he did know Emily. If she vouched for her brother, then everything would be okay.

Or at least, Sean hoped so. It did sound like Peter was having a hard time, but he wasn't alone, even though he didn't know it yet.

Peter was sitting on a short half-wall on the other side of the street from his building, staring at his phone, when Emily called him back. He continued staring, wary of answering. For whatever reason, he didn't want to know what she was about to tell him.

He'd panicked when he'd called her earlier. He didn't have a lot of friends — actually, he didn't have *any* friends. He had people he was friendly with, but he knew he couldn't call them and ask them for a place to stay or a job. His sister, on the other hand, was his sister. They'd grown up together, and they'd always been close. He'd hoped she could help him, at least with a place for the night, but now he was afraid to answer in case she couldn't.

What would he do if she couldn't help him? Where would he spend the night? He had some savings, so he could get a hotel, but it wouldn't last long. He also had to find a job, and he didn't know where to start, not with his personal computer and everything else under water in his apartment.

It hadn't just flooded. The pipe had exploded right in Peter's living room. The pressure had destroyed the wall, and from what he'd been told, it had ruined everything that was in there. He hadn't seen the place yet because the firefighters hadn't allowed him inside, but he already knew from the way they looked at him with pity that there wouldn't be a lot he could save. That was yet another problem, and a problem he didn't know how to solve.

He sucked in a breath and answered. "Please tell me you found a couch I can sleep on tonight."

"I did better than that. I found you a job and a bedroom where you can stay for as long as you need to."

Peter was relieved for all of five seconds. Then, he narrowed his eyes. "That sounds too good to be true. What are the conditions?"

"No conditions. It's not in Boston, though. You're going to have to move."

Peter closed his eyes and swallowed. It was better than he'd expected. It wasn't like he loved living here anyway. He was here because it was where he'd gone to college and where he'd found his first job, and he'd stayed here because, well, it was what he knew and what he'd known for the past several years. He didn't have family, though. Emily had moved when she'd graduated and was working in another city.

What would Peter be leaving behind if he left? Not much — a flooded apartment, a job he'd just lost. He had a few friends he would miss, but that was it.

He sighed. "Tell me."

"I called Sean."

Peter rolled his eyes. "Of course you did." Emily and Sean had been best friends since college, and they were so close that Peter had always wondered if there was more between them than friendship. He'd never met Sean, though. Their schedule had never fit together when Sean and Emily had been in college, and that was fine. Or at least, it had been fine until now. Since it seemed that Sean was giving Peter everything he needed, though, he wished he knew him better.

"Who else did you expect me to call?" Emily asked. "He's

always been there when I was in trouble, and today isn't any different. He's offering you his guest room and a job. It won't be as an accountant, though."

Peter bit his lower lip. "What kind of job is he offering, then?"

"He owns a construction company. Most of his family is in that line of work. His father was before him, and one of his brothers builds furniture."

"Construction? Can you imagine me working in construction?"

"I can't, but it's the only thing he has available. You can say no if you want, Peter. I did what I could, but I understand it's not what you expected."

Peter *couldn't* say no. He didn't want to sound ungrateful, but more importantly, he couldn't afford to. He needed a job and a place to stay, and this was the easiest way to get that. He felt slightly guilty — he was an adult, and he should be able to find a job on his own. He was down on his luck, though, and he felt like he was drowning along with all this stuff. He needed help, no matter how little he liked admitting it. He liked it even less that Emily had called Sean to get that help, but really, he should have guessed she would. She always called Sean when she had a problem, and this time wasn't any different.

"It will help you get back on your feet," Emily murmured. "He's a good man, Peter. I know you don't know him and that you're slightly wary of him, but I promise you that he'll do everything he can for you."

"I don't understand why," Peter admitted.

"He's not like us, like our family. I know we've always had each other's back, but it's only us. Sean has a big family, though. He has six brothers, and they've always been there for each other, as have their parents. I'm part of his family, too, which means he'll do everything he can to help me, and through me, you."

"Even though he doesn't know me?"

"I vouched for you. He trusts me. He wants to help you. Allow him to do that, please. I don't know who else to call. I want to do what I can for you, but I don't think there's anything else in my power."

Peter couldn't say no. "I'll go."

Emily sounded relieved. "Good. I'll text you his address and his phone number. He's expecting a call from you."

"How far away does he live?"

"I'm guessing it's going to take you four or five hours by car. That's how long it took him to go home for the holidays and stuff when we were in college. You still have your car, don't you?"

"It's the *only* thing I still have." Peter regretted his words right away. With how his life was going, he was going to break down or something like that.

"All right. See what you can save from your apartment and go to Sean."

"Thank you."

"You don't have to thank me. We're family."

That much was true. He and Emily were closer now than they'd been as children, and while she'd been the only one Peter could call for help, he hadn't truly expected her to do anything. Instead, she'd found him a place to stay and a job. He didn't care if he had to build walls or something like that. He would do what he had to do to survive.

They hung up, and a few seconds later, his phone trilled with a text. It was the information Emily had promised to send, and Peter stared at the address on the screen.

Emily was right. It was going to take him at least five hours to drive there. It was a small town, too, so it would be a change of scenery. Maybe that was what he needed. Living in the city on his own hadn't worked. None of it was his fault, but he had a chance at a new start, and he wanted to take it.

He got to his feet and looked at the building, then at the firefighters still milling around. He needed to grab the few things that had survived the flooding — if anything had — and then he would leave. He had to talk to the firefighters. They wouldn't let him inside on his own, and he understood why. He wanted to leave all of this behind, and the sooner he did it, the better it would be. His life had flipped upside down in one afternoon, and he was lost. He didn't know if he would be able to find a way forward, but Emily's help had been a good start. He didn't have anything to stay for, but a lot to leave behind.

Sean was still thinking about Peter when he got to his parents' home. He felt sorry for the guy, even though he'd never met him. He was glad he could do something to help, but he was a bit worried. He only knew what Emily told him to go by. He wasn't sure why he and Peter had never met when he thought about it. Emily had spent several Christmases with Sean and his family when they were younger. She and Sean saw each other several times a year. Peter was never around, though. The fact that Emily and Peter lived in different cities probably had a lot to do with that, and the fact that Sean lived in a small town also did. Still, Sean was both wary and excited to meet Peter. He'd heard Emily talk about her brother for years, and he was curious about the guy. He sounded sweet and obviously down on his luck. If there was anything Sean could do to help him, he was eager to do just that.

He parked his truck in front of his parents' house and got out. From the cars already there, he could tell his twin brother was there, as was his mate, probably. Jack also was there, and maybe Andy had come along with him. That would mean spending the evening with three of his brothers and one of his brothers' mates, and Sean wasn't looking forward to having that many people around. He was tired, and he'd expected a quiet evening with his family. There would be no quiet if so many of his brothers were together, especially with Jack and Andy there.

He was lucky. Andy was out on a date, so only Jack had come. That meant there were only three of them.

Sean's mom smiled at him when she saw him and hugged him, then pushed him to the bathroom to wash his hands. Sean went, still smiling. He always smiled when he was home. It was familiar, and it felt good. He also liked seeing Hugh being so happy with his mate. He hadn't known what to think of Leon the first time he'd met him, but he was glad Leon and his brother had found each other. They both deserved to be happy, and they were, blissfully so.

"What's new with you?" Hugo asked as the two of them set the table.

Leon and Jack were in the living room, along with Sean's dad. Sean's mom was in the kitchen, putting the last touches on dinner. It felt like Sean had gone back in time to when he was a teenager, and it was soothing. Sometimes he still wished he were a teenager. He wouldn't have to worry about bills, finding jobs, and putting enough money away for rainy days. He couldn't help but think about that when he thought about Peter. The poor man had lost everything, so even if he had some savings, they probably wouldn't last long. That made him feel better about giving Peter a job and a place to stay.

"Emily called earlier," Sean said.

Hugh's face lit up. "Is she coming to visit?"

"No. She needed help for her brother. Poor guy lost his job *and* his apartment today."

"I bet you gave him a job."

"And I offered him my guest room. He's going to be

staying with me for a bit."

Hugh frowned. "You've never met him, though, have you?"

"I haven't. But he's Emily's brother. He's down on his luck, and I can't abandon him."

"What happened to him?" Sean's mom asked as she walked into the dining room.

Sean explained to her about Peter losing his job and his apartment, and he could tell from her expression that she was worried. For whom, he didn't know, but he'd find out soon enough.

"That poor man. Is he okay? When will he get here? You have to give him at least a week of vacation before he starts working, Sean. After everything that happened to him, he's going to need time to buy new things, and more importantly, to wrap his mind around how much his life has changed."

Sean hadn't even thought about it, and he was grateful his mom had. "I'll tell him that." Although if Peter was anything like Sean, he would want to start working right away. It would probably take some convincing for him to take vacation days, especially since he hadn't even started the job yet. Sean would pay him for that week, though. He always gave his people paid vacations, and Peter wouldn't be any different if Sean hired him.

"That's good. You'll have to bring him around. He's going to need family."

"He has Emily."

"That's not what I meant. He needs a mother."

Emily's parents had never been accepting, neither of her or of Peter. They hadn't liked that Emily had wanted to go to college and that she was a lawyer, and they liked that Peter was gay even less. Emily had cried on Sean's shoulder more than once when they were younger, and she still did sometimes. She didn't understand why her parents thought that instead of being a lawyer, she should have found herself a nice husband and had kids. She didn't understand why they'd decided they didn't have a son when they found out Peter was gay.

Sean didn't understand, either. His parents had never cared about who he and his brothers dated. Hell, both Hugh and Curtis had found their mates, and both mates were male. Yet their parents still hadn't kicked them out. They welcomed their mates, and the family had grown. They would never even think about kicking them out for who they loved or what they did with their lives.

So no, Sean didn't understand, but he did know how lucky he was. He also realized that his mom was going to adopt Peter. As soon as she got her hands on him, he would be overwhelmed, but he'd be part of the family. That was fine. Emily already was, and it was about time her brother became family, too.

"I'll tell him about you guys. It's going to be overwhelming to meet all of us at once, though," Sean said, as he and his mom sat at the table.

Hugh called the rest of their family, and they started entering the dining room.

"Then you have to bring him to dinner with just the four of us. I know he doesn't have a big family, so it's understandable that he'll be overwhelmed."

Leon snorted as he sat on her other side. "Big family is an understatement when it comes to you guys. I still don't know how you survived having seven boys."

Sean's mom laughed. "After I had twins, everything came easy. They were the most work."

Leon's eyes twinkled when he looked at Hugh. "I bet. They're still a lot of work now, aren't they? There always seems to be at least a few of them around when I come here."

Sean's mom smiled softly. "Some, but I'm more than happy

to have them home. I've always wanted a big family, and I got what I wished for."

"And I heard you're taking on someone else."

"That's not a problem. Eventually, I hope all my sons will meet their mates. That will make fourteen people, and it's more than fine with me." She paused and looked at Hugh. "More people, if any of you start having children."

Curtis and his mate weren't talking about having kids as far as Sean knew, and since they weren't here tonight, their mom's focus was all on the Leon and Curtis. Leon seemed to find the situation hilarious, while Hugh was looking anywhere but at him or their mom.

"We're not talking about having kids yet," Leon said. "Maybe in a few years? I don't know. I never thought I'd find love, let alone a family."

Sean's mom reached for his hand and patted it. "But you do. I'm glad you feel safe with us."

For some reason, Sean found himself hoping that Peter would feel the same way. He needed help, and Sean's family was willing to give it to him. Hopefully, he would see it as what it was — family helping family — and not as charity. Sean couldn't do anything about it right now, though, so he turned his attention to his plate. He'd have enough time to worry about him once Peter called to tell him he was coming, and when he got here, things really would get started.

Sean thought like his mom, though. The more, the merrier. What was one more family member when there were already eleven of them, twelve if he counted Emily?

CHAPTER TWO

Peter was so close he could taste it. He'd been traveling most of the night, only stopping to sleep a few hours until the sun came up. He hadn't been able to save a lot of his stuff, although his bedroom hadn't been as severely hit as the living room and the rest of the apartment. He had some clothes, and luckily for him, his computer had been in the bedroom, so he'd saved that and a few personal items, like pictures and books. He also had toiletries, but that was about it, and while he felt bad about it, he also felt *free*. He didn't know why, but leaving almost all the things he'd acquired over the past several years felt like he genuinely had a new start.

Maybe that was what he needed. Maybe that was why fate had taken away his job and his apartment.

And now, it sounded like it was going to take his car away from him, too.

It made a strange noise, almost as if the engine had fallen off and Peter had left it somewhere down the road. Then there was a small bang, and smoke started coming out of the front of the car. Peter knew he had to pull over, but he didn't want to. He was close to town, but not close enough. He would have to walk if he didn't manage to get his car closer, and he wasn't looking forward to it since it was raining.

It looked like he wasn't going to have a choice.

The car stopped on its own. The only thing Peter could do was steer it toward the edge of the road. Then, he stared at it from the driver seat. His eyes prickled, and he felt like he was about to cry.

What had he done? Why was all of this happening to him? Had he offended someone up there? He didn't believe in God, but he didn't care if other people did. Maybe that was his offense. Maybe he should have believed.

He slammed his hands on the steering wheel, once, twice, but it didn't help. A mixture of sadness, rage, and other feelings boiled in his chest. A tear rolled down his cheek, but he angrily whipped it away.

It was what it was. There was nothing he could do to fix it, at least not when it came to his job and apartment. He *could* fix this, though — hopefully.

He didn't know what he was getting himself into, being a city boy in a small town, but this didn't bode well for the future. He also didn't know who to call. He couldn't call Emily, who wasn't even here, and the only other useful number he had was Sean's. Sean was the one who was closest to him right now, and Peter prayed he wouldn't mind picking him up. If he did, well, Peter supposed that would show him what their future relationship would be like.

He took his phone from the passenger seat where he'd put it as he listened to the GPS. His hands shook. He didn't like talking on the phone, mostly because it made him anxious, but he had to force himself to do it. The only other option for him was to stay right where he was and hope someone would pass by. He supposed he could also find a mechanic in town, but it would be easier and faster for him to ask Sean about it.

The phone rang, and Peter waited. He thought Sean wasn't going to answer until he heard, "Hello?"

Sean sounded out of breath. Peter was curious as to what he'd been doing, but he didn't ask. "Sean? It's Peter, Emily's brother."

"Of course. Are you in town? Are you looking for my apartment?"

"Uh, no." Peter looked around. He wasn't in town, even

though he'd passed a *Welcome to Clarkstown* sign a while ago. There was a tiny mall to the right, but that was about it. "My car broke down. I don't know where I am exactly, although my GPS said it would be fifteen minutes before I got to town."

There was a pause, then Sean asked, "Your car actually broke down?"

"There's smoke coming out of the engine, but I managed to steer it to the side of the road. Can you help me? Maybe give me the number of a mechanic in town? I can call them myself."

"Don't worry about that. Stay put, and I'll be right there."

Peter slumped against the seat. "I can call."

"You don't have to. I'll call the mechanic if you send me the GPS coordinates, so he knows where you are. I don't know how long it'll take him to get there, though."

"Well, there's not much around here, but I see a coffee shop. There's a short row of shops close by, and the coffee shop is called Java Fix."

To Peter's surprise, Sean chuckled. "That would be the coffee shop where my brother works. You should walk there. I know where you are, and you can get some coffee while the mechanic and I get to you. Unless you don't have an umbrella?"

Peter didn't, but right now, he wanted nothing more than leave his car. "I'll make do. Thanks for asking, though."

"You're Emily's brother. You're family. Of course I worry." He paused. "And by the way, my mom wants to meet you."

Peter blinked. "Your mom?"

"Yep. She raised seven sons, and she kind of adopted Emily when I brought her home. You know, her being a girl and everything. And now she knows Emily's brother is in trouble, and she wants to do the same with you. You'll see when you meet her."

Peter wasn't sure he wanted to. Sean's words both petrified

him and made him strangely happy.

He and Sean said goodbye, and Peter hung up. He stared at the smoke still coming out of the engine, thinking about Sean's words.

He didn't understand why Sean's mother seemed so excited to meet him. Maybe it was because his own mother had never been a very loving person. They weren't a touchy-feely family. She'd never hugged him much, or kissed him, or even told him she loved him. Then she'd kicked him out when he'd come out. Well, she'd nodded along while his father told him that he wasn't welcome in their home anymore, not unless he made better life choices. It hadn't been quite as dramatic as kicking him out, especially since he'd already been going to college and he had his own place, but still. He'd lost his family that night, except for his sister, and he'd never thought he would get another one.

He couldn't think he would, though. He wasn't here to find a family. He was here to work, put money in his savings, and decide what was next for him. The job and the apartment Sean was offering were temporary. Peter didn't know what would happen after that, and he didn't want to think about it right now, but it wouldn't be forever.

He sucked in a breath, put his phone in his pocket, and opened the door. Luckily for him, the rain had slowed down to a drizzle, so even though he was damp when he got to the coffee shop, it wasn't a disaster. He shook his head, pushing his hair out of his eyes, and looked around as he stepped in.

The place was warm and smelled of coffee and sugar. All the furniture inside seemed to be made of wood, both light and dark. It was cozy, and Peter relaxed immediately. It wasn't home, but it felt like it.

A young guy behind the counter eyed him. Peter didn't know if this was Sean's brother, but he wasn't about to ask. He strode toward the counter, looking at the list of coffees on the slate behind the barista. "I'll just have an espresso," he said, forcing himself to smile and hoping it looked human.

Laurie—the name was on the nametag—smiled back and leaned over the counter. "You're new here, aren't you? I've never seen you around."

"Is the town so small that you know everyone?"

Laurie shrugged. "Maybe not everyone, but I would remember a guy as cute as you."

Peter felt his cheeks heat, and he looked away.

Laurie chuckled, but it wasn't mean. "I'm Laurie," he said.

"Peter."

"Well, Peter. Are you new in town, then?"

"I am."

Peter was grateful when he heard the door open behind him, but Laurie wasn't. He looked behind Peter and groaned. "What are *you* doing here?" he asked.

"None of your business, little brother," a strong male voice answered.

Laurie was flirting. Sean knew his brother well enough to be able to see that, and he was pretty sure that the man his brother was flirting with was Peter.

Peter, of whom he'd only seen the back of for now. It was enough to tell him that Peter was tall, probably around six-feet-something, and that he had shaggy dark-blond hair. He was well-built, at least from behind, and Sean didn't even bother trying not to look at his ass.

And what an ass it was. Round, high, encased in jeans, calling for Sean's hands.

Sean forced himself to focus on Peter the man rather than on his ass. Laurie was glaring at Sean, probably thinking he'd interrupted his flirting because he wanted to be mean. He couldn't be further from the truth, though. He was here for

Peter, and he was amused.

Peter turned around, and yep, he was just as gorgeous as Sean suspected. His eyes were a warm brown, although his gaze was troubled right now. His nose was straight and small, and while his front teeth were slightly crooked, Sean thought it added to Peter's charm.

Peter smiled, and it illuminated his entire face. Hell, it illuminated the whole coffee shop, and Sean couldn't help but smile back. "Peter?" he asked as he got closer.

Peter nodded. "I guess you're Sean?"

Sean was close enough, so he offered Peter his hand. Peter took it and shook it, and he froze at the same moment as Sean.

Sean wanted to lean closer. It was possible that the scent came from someone else, but he doubted it. It *had* to come from Peter, who was the person closest to Sean. Besides, the coffee shop was almost empty. There was a possibility that one of the women in the corner smelled like Sean's mate, but Sean doubted it. He'd dated a few girls in his time, but lately, he'd been focused on guys—when he dated at all. It didn't happen often, not when he was busy with work.

But he'd smelled his mate. He couldn't deny that, and he found himself hoping it was Peter. He licked his lips, still staring. "Can you smell it?"

Peter bit his lower lip and peeked at Laurie. "I can. Should we go outside?" he asked in a soft voice.

"Whatever you need to do, you can do it inside," Laurie snapped. "Here's your coffee, Peter." He turned his attention to Sean. "What do you want? Are you checking in on me?"

Peter looked confused. He dropped Sean's hand, and Sean wanted to take it back. He didn't, focusing on his brother who was in a snit instead. "The world doesn't revolve around you, Laurie. I'm not here to check on you. I'm here to pick up Peter."

Laurie's gaze moved from Sean to Peter. "You know him?"

"He's Emily's brother. He'll be staying with me for a while. You'd know that if you bothered calling or even texting." There were fourteen years between the two of them, and Laurie was young, but they were still family, and they'd always gotten along. It hurt a bit to be an afterthought for Laurie.

"Trust you to already have a hold on the new cute guy."

Peter's cheeks flushed, and Sean found it adorable. "It's not like you think," he started, trying to explain.

Laurie shrugged and stepped away. "I don't want to hear it. Just go, will you? I don't want to work with my brother peering over my shoulder." His expression softened when he turned to Peter. "Welcome to town. I didn't know you were Emily's brother, and I'm sorry I made you uncomfortable."

"You didn't. Thank you for the coffee."

"It's on the house. And I'm sure I'll see you soon enough. If you're Emily's brother and you're going to stay in town, you're going to be invited to our home more than once."

Sean softly sorted. "You'd have to be there to see him, though," he pointed out.

Laurie's huffed. "Did Mom send you?"

"She didn't, but I know she misses you." Although since Laurie was only nineteen, she didn't expect much from him. All of them had needed their space when they were in their early twenties. At thirty-five, Sean was old enough to know that his family and his parents were important to him, but at nineteen, he'd left them behind to focus on his friends and his own life.

"Call Mom." He gestured at the door so Peter would follow him.

It was still drizzling, but Sean felt better once he could take a deep breath. He did so and turned to Peter, who had wrapped his hands around his coffee. They were under the coffee shop awning, so they weren't getting wet, but the air felt damp, and it made Peter's hair curl at the bottom.

"Do you think we should smell each other better?" Sean asked. He desperately wanted to, but he didn't want to make Peter uncomfortable.

Peter looked at him. "I suppose we should. At least we'll know for sure."

Sean was happy, but he still kept his distance. He leaned closer, close enough that he could brush his nose against Peter's cheek. Then, he inhaled, and he heard Peter do the same.

Peter spluttered, while Sean sucked in a breath. They were mates, all right. Peter's scent wrapped around Sean, making him feel at home and loved. He'd never felt anything like it, or anything that made his swan settle the way it just had.

"I didn't expect this," Sean said as he leaned back.

"I didn't, either. Finding my mate was the furthest thing from my mind when I agreed to come here," Peter said. He looked away.

Sean followed his gaze and noticed his car on the side of the road. The mechanic still hadn't arrived, but it wouldn't be long before he did.

"If I'd known Emily's brother was my mate, I would have asked to meet you a long time ago," he said.

"We couldn't know. I'm surprised it's happening now."

"Maybe that's why you lost your job and the apartment," Sean said. "Or maybe meeting me now is the result of that happening." He truly believed that shifters met their mates when they most needed them, and that fate had gotten them together.

His brother Curtis had met his mate when he'd been unconscious in the snow, completely naked. An animal had tried to eat him while he was in his swan form, and Manuel had come to the rescue and had taken Curtis home before he could die of exposure.

Sean's twin had also met his mate in a moment in which he wasn't sure what he was doing with his life. Hugh had always been a loner, much more than Sean, but he'd still managed to meet Leon, and thankfully, they'd worked things out. It hadn't been easy, with their clashing personalities, but they were happy now, and it gave Sean hope that he and Peter could make it work, too.

He wanted to. He was thirty-five, and while he'd never really thought about settling down, he wanted to. He wanted a family, possibly children. More importantly, he wanted someone to wake up with every morning, someone who would smile at him and hold him, someone who would be there for him when he needed them. He wanted a partner, and now, fate had dumped his mate into his lap.

It couldn't be that easy, but he wanted it to be. He wanted things to be easy between him and Peter, but he didn't know if that would be the case. Whatever had happened to Peter, it was obvious that losing his job and his apartment, and now his car, had overwhelmed him and made him feel lost. Sean wanted to help him and get closer to him. He wasn't sure Peter would let him, though.

This was *not* what Peter had expected when he'd arrived in Clarkstown, and he didn't know what to do or say. Sean was peering at him, probably wondering what was next, and Peter was right there with him. He didn't *know* what was next.

He was supposed to move in with Sean, to get to know him as a friend and his boss, and as soon as he had enough money in his savings account, leave town. That wasn't going to be possible right now, and probably never.

Because Sean and Peter were mates.

At least they were both shifters. That way, Peter wouldn't have to explain what being mates meant, that shifters were real, that they were supposed to spend the rest of their lives together. No, Sean already knew all of that, and so did Peter.

That wasn't as helpful as Peter had hoped it would be, though. Yes, both he and Sean knew what was going on, but it was still confusing. Why had he met Sean now? Had Sean always been his mate? If they'd met before, would they have been together for years already?

All those questions were moot. Peter would never get answers to them, and he didn't want them, not really. He didn't think they mattered. The only thing that did was that he and Sean were mates and that Peter was supposed to move in with Sean and work under him for the next several months.

Under him. Peter's cheeks flushed, and he looked away. He hadn't meant anything when he'd thought that, but now he couldn't stop thinking about him being under Sean quite literally, possibly in bed, although he wouldn't mind a couch, either. He had to stop thinking with his cock and focus on what was going on, even though he wasn't sure what that was.

He rubbed his face with his free hand. "I'm sorry about your brother. I mean, I wasn't flirting with him. It was never my intention."

Sean was still smiling, thankfully. "Don't worry about that. Laurie's a flirt. We all know it, and besides, he didn't know you were my mate. I didn't, either. I'm not angry at you, if that's what you think."

"Thank you."

Sean cocked his head. "Has anyone ever been angry at you for talking to another guy?"

Peter wasn't proud of it, but it had happened. "One of my exes. He's been an ex for a while for that reason."

"Good. Because I don't care who you talk to, Peter. We're not together, not yet, and even when we are, I won't control you. Being in a relationship means that you trust the other person, and *that* means that you don't have anything against them talking to other people." He paused. "Of course, it doesn't mean we'll ever have a relationship. The fact that we're mates doesn't mean we have to end up together."

Peter bit his lower lip and looked away. He didn't like where this was going. He wasn't sure whether Sean was giving him an out or giving himself one. "Being mates *does* mean that we belong together," he pointed out softly.

"True, although I've always wondered who decides that. It's not what I was getting to, though. I'm more than willing to give this a try, but I don't expect anything from you. I know you're down on your luck, and I truly just want to help you. If something comes out of that, I'll be happy. If it doesn't, and you decide that you're not made for small-town life and that you want to go back to Boston once you're back on your feet, I won't argue."

Peter stayed silent. He *wanted* Sean to protest. He wanted him to want to be with him, to want to keep him close. Along with Emily, Sean should be the one person who wanted Peter close, yet he sounded like he wasn't exactly happy to find out that Peter was his mate.

Peter realized it was because they'd just met, and they didn't know each other. It hurt, but he had to push that pain away. It wasn't a personal rejection, not yet. Sean was saying all the right things, and Peter would have realized that sooner if he'd been in his right mind.

He cleared his throat. "I wanted to thank you," he started.

"There's nothing to thank me for."

"There is. You don't even know me, yet you offered me a place to stay and a job. I know you did it because I'm Emily's brother, but still. Thank you. You're the only person who agreed to help, and I don't know where I would be if you hadn't."

Sean turned to face him. He was smiling softly, and Peter found himself smiling back. "Well, you'd probably be splashing around your apartment right now," Sean said.

For whatever reason, Peter smiled more widely. "Proba-bly." He sighed heavily. "God, everything is such a mess."

"Are you feeling okay?" Sean asked. He reached for Peter, but Peter expected him to stop before they touched.

He didn't. Instead, he gently touched Peter's shoulder. When Peter didn't protest, he cupped and squeezed it, and Peter broke down.

He wasn't proud of it, but he also wasn't ashamed of it. If Sean had anything to say about the fact that Peter was crying, it meant that even though they were mates, he wasn't the per-fect man for Peter.

Peter reached up and dried the tears from his cheeks. "I'm sorry," he said. He might not be ashamed of crying, but he didn't want to make Sean uncomfortable. "It's just so much, you know? I was let go from my job, my apartment flooded, my car broke down, and now there's you. I don't even know where to start."

"How about you start by walking to my truck with me? I can drive you back to your car, where you can gather your stuff and put it in the back. Then we'll wait for the mechanic. Once he tows your car away, I'll take you home."

Sean sounded reasonable, steady, and strong, and Peter found himself leaning toward him. It was the only thing that could be done right now. Peter was freaking out, but there wasn't an easy solution. He should stop thinking about how he'd been fired and that he'd lost everything he'd accumu-lated in his life. It was what it was, and he should focus on the future. Even though his life had been flipped upside down, he was okay. He had a new job lined up, a rent-free room in Sean's apartment, and he was sure that the mechanic would manage to fix his car — or at least, he prayed that was the case. He didn't know what he would do otherwise, and he didn't want to think about it.

He also had a mate. He didn't know what it meant, either

for him or for Sean, but they would find out eventually. They were going to have to share an apartment for some time, and Peter hoped it meant they would get to know each other. He also hoped they would fall in love.

Because if this was the only thing that came out of his life being a wreck, he would be okay with it. If being fired and losing everything he owned, including his car, meant that at the end of it, he had his mate, he would go through it again and again.

He wouldn't enjoy it, though.

He rubbed his eyes, wishing he hadn't started crying in front of Sean. "That sounds like a plan. Thank you."

"You're going to have to stop doing that," Sean pointed out.

"Doing what?" Peter asked even though he suspected he knew what Sean was talking about.

"Thanking me. I already told you, there's nothing to thank me for. You're family, much more than I realized. I would have done this for you even if you were only Emily's brother. The fact that you're my mate doesn't change anything, not right now. You'll stay with me, and you'll work for me. We can figure out everything else once you're settled."

"You truly don't expect anything from me?" Peter wasn't sure he liked it.

"I don't know, Peter. I think we should talk about it, about what our expectations are. I'm just not sure this is the right moment for you to do that."

Peter couldn't say he was wrong. He was already overwhelmed as it was. Could he add a conversation about his mate and their future together to the mountain of things he had to think about?

Sean already had a soft spot for Peter, and he wasn't

surprised. His mate was overwhelmed and fragile, something that was entirely understandable with everything that had happened to him, and it triggered Sean's protective instinct.

Which made him realize he should be taking better care of his mate.

He promised himself he would do better. They had to talk, but they didn't have to do it in front of the coffee shop with people walking in and out behind them.

He gently put a hand on Peter's elbow, then turned him toward his truck. "Why don't we sit down? Are you going to drink that coffee?"

Peter looked at the cup he was still holding as if he was surprised it was in his hand. "I think so. I'm kind of cold."

It wasn't cold, so Sean suspected that Peter felt that way more because of the shock than anything else. "Drink it. We can sit in my truck when you're done."

Peter nodded. He looked a bit dazed, but he obeyed, drinking his espresso. Then, he stood holding the empty cup, looking lost.

Sean took it from his hand and threw it away, then steered Peter toward the truck. Peter moved without objection.

Once there, he opened the passenger door, helping Peter inside. When Peter was seated, Sean took one of the bottles of water he always kept in the back seat and offered it to him. "Here you go," he said.

Peter blinked at the water. "Why are you giving me that?"

"Honestly? I'm not sure. Isn't that what people give other people when they're in shock?"

Peter's eyes widened. "I'm not in shock. I promise. I'm fine."

"You might not be in shock, but you're understandably all over the place. It's not a bad thing, considering everything that happened to you in the past few days, and I'm not berating you for it. I'm just trying to take care of you."

He would have even if Peter weren't his mate. All that had happened to Peter — getting fired, losing his apartment and everything in it, his car breaking down — would have been a lot for anyone. Sean was glad he could take care of Peter and try to make him feel better. He didn't know if those disasters had happened because they were fated to meet now, or if they'd met now because Peter's life was a mess, but whatever the reason, whichever way it went, Sean was going to take care of his mate.

It was his duty. It would be his pleasure.

He almost couldn't believe he'd met his mate. He hadn't expected it to happen, not right after both Curtis and Hugh had found theirs. The three of them were the oldest of the brothers, and since it was rare for shifters to meet their mates, Sean had thought he was out of luck when it came to that. If two of his brothers had met theirs, there was no way he would find his.

He'd been wrong.

He looked at Peter, who was finally relaxing. He appeared defeated, and Sean reached out, not thinking too much about what he was doing. He stroked his thumb onto Peter's cheekbone, drying the tears that were still lingering there. Peter's eyes widened and he stared at Sean, but he didn't pull away.

"I don't want you to feel bad about everything that's happened," Sean murmured. "None of it was your fault. And now, you're home. You don't have to worry about any of that again."

Peter wrinkled his nose. "I'm not actually home, though."

He was right. He wasn't. His home was in Boston, not in Clarkstown. Sean hoped that eventually, though, it would become home for Peter and that *he* would, too.

He wanted to be Peter's home, to be who Peter came back to at night. He doubted that Peter would work for him for a long time, but that wasn't a problem, because he wasn't planning on letting Peter move out of his apartment once he was there.

His brothers always made fun of him because he had an apartment rather than a house. He owned a construction company, yet he chose to live in a cramped place instead of building his own home or maybe flipping one. He'd done that on purpose, though.

Sean hadn't expected to meet his mate, but he'd known that eventually, he would meet someone he would fall in love with. He would maybe get married. And together, he and his husband would find a house that fit both of them. They would make it the perfect place for both of them instead of just Sean, a place where they could grow old and raise a family.

And that man was Peter.

Sean had to be careful not to get too much ahead of himself, though. Peter might be his mate, and they might belong together, but that didn't mean things would be smooth sailing. He hoped they would, but he knew better.

He couldn't push, not on this. He had to give Peter time to get used to his new life, to wrap his mind around everything he'd lost and everything he'd gained. If he did that, Peter would feel at home here.

It would be hard not to push, not to try to hold Peter when he needed it, not to kiss him senseless to distract him. Sean promised himself he would anyway. Peter had to be the one to take the next step. They knew they were mates, and they had to talk about it, but that wasn't all when it came to Peter. He had to get used to having a new home, a new job, and possibly needing a new car. Sean couldn't rush ahead when it came to their relationship and their future.

Peter rubbed his face, took a sip of water, then looked at Sean. "Okay. Let's talk."

"We don't have to do that now."

"Maybe I'm not ready to get in deep, but I do think I want

to know what's going to happen next. The fact that we're mates changes everything."

"It doesn't have to. You still have a job with my company and a place to stay in my guest room. That's all you need to focus on for now."

"There's no way you don't want anything from me, though. We're mates. You *have* to want something."

"Like I said, there's no rush. You can get used to this new life of yours before we talk about it."

Something glinted in Peter's gaze, and he crossed his arms over his chest. He glared at Sean.

Instead of finding him intimidating, Sean found him adorable.

"What if I *want* to talk about it?" Peter's expression softened. "I know this is confusing. Trust me. I need to know what's going to happen, though. I don't want more surprises, not ever again, if at all possible. I need to know what you expect from me, and for you to know what I expect from you."

"I'm listening." Sean should have realized this was why Peter was pushing. Of course he didn't want surprises. The last three had been horrible.

Peter's shoulders relaxed. "Well, I don't know if I like you. We just met. But I know you're my sister's best friend, and I trust Emily. So I guess I'm not opposed to dating you."

Sean barked out a laugh. "You guess you're not opposed?"

"You know what I mean. Some people jump into bed and into a relationship with their mates right away, but I don't think I'm ready for that. I don't think I'm ready for much, to be honest. But I *do* want to try to date you. Once I settle down, I think we should try that. If you're okay with it, of course."

Sean was more than okay with it. "We can do that. I don't want to rush you into anything. I understand that your life is a mess right now, and I don't want to add to it. That's the only reason I wanted to wait to talk."

Peter stared at him for a moment, then nodded. "I understand, but I *don't* want surprises. Besides, I don't think your addition to my life makes it more of a mess. If anything, it's the only good thing that's come out of this."

Sean hoped that was true. He wanted Peter to be right. He wanted to give him everything he wanted and needed.

And since he thought he couldn't, at least for now, it was another promise he made himself. He would give Peter time and space, but not too much. Peter wasn't wrong. They were mates, and they would have to learn to deal with that. The best way to do it seemed to be to date and see where things went, and if that was what Peter wanted, it was what would happen.

CHAPTER THREE

Things were, well, kind of awkward. Even though Peter and Sean were mates and they lived together, Peter wasn't sure how to behave.

This wasn't his apartment. He was only a guest here, even though Sean didn't treat him like one. Sean acted as if they were together, but they hadn't even gone on their first date yet, and Peter was lost. He also didn't know how to take Sean's offer to take a week off the job to get used to his new life. He'd thought he would start the day after he arrived, but instead, Sean had told him no. He was still paying Peter, something that made Peter both happy, because he needed the money, and uncomfortable. He was being paid for doing nothing, and he was being paid by his mate. It didn't matter that Sean had said he and his team were finishing up a job and that it would be better for Peter to come in once they started a new one — Peter felt awkward.

So today he would get breakfast ready. It was his first day of work after an entire week, and he wondered how he was supposed to behave with Sean. He knew that on the job he shouldn't treat Sean as his mate, but then, he hadn't treated Sean as his mate even when they weren't on the job. They *were* mates, but they didn't know each other yet. They lived together already, though, and Sean had given Peter a job and a place to stay.

It was confusing, and Peter wished it wasn't.

Was it so bad to accept what his mate was willingly offering and for people to know what they were to each other? It

36

might be when it came to the job. Peter didn't know the people he was going to work with, but Sean did, so he would follow his lead.

It wouldn't be hard to keep himself in check anyway. Even though they'd been living together, they weren't acting like mates. He knew Sean was giving him the time and space he needed to get used to this new life, but some days, he wished Sean didn't. He wanted Sean to grab him and kiss him. He wanted Sean to tell him everything would be okay, and he wanted those words to be true.

Everything would probably be okay, but Peter was going to have to take things into his own hands. It was kind of terrifying, especially after everything he'd been through, but he could do it.

Hopefully.

He flipped the pancake in the pan, poked at it for a moment, then slid it onto the pile he already had on a plate. He'd gotten up earlier than he should have so he could cook breakfast. It was the least he could do for Sean, and he hoped Sean wouldn't mind. It was his kitchen after all, and he didn't even know Peter could cook.

The main reason he didn't know was that he hadn't allowed Peter to cook yet. He'd been coddling Peter, and Peter knew it. It was over now, though. Even though he hadn't been happy with it, Peter had been grateful for the week of respite. He'd been able to settle down while Sean was at work, to make the apartment just a little bit his. He'd been careful not to invade the communal spaces, but the guestroom he was staying in felt like his place now, and that would have to do. He'd also called his sister more often than in the past few years. They'd talked a lot, mostly about Sean, but also about what was next for Peter. She was over-the-moon-happy for both of them, and she wanted to visit, but Peter was grateful that she was busy right now. He wanted time alone with Sean, even though he didn't know what to do with it. He wanted them to start dating, to truly be mates, but he didn't know how to ask for that.

"What's that smell?" Sean asked as he shuffled his feet into the kitchen. He was only wearing pajama pants, and he was rubbing his face. His hair was all over the place. It shot up on one side, while the other lay flat against his head.

It was adorable—and hot. Peter could imagine this was what Sean would look like in the morning when they finally got to wake up next to each other, and he had to bite his lower lip against the impulse to reach out to touch him.

Sean wasn't a man Peter would have thought of as adorable in any other circumstances, but in this case, it was the right word for it. Sean was obviously sleepy, and he froze as he took in the feast Peter had prepared. He stared at the small table in the kitchen, his eyes wide, his mouth open, his hair still spiky on one side and flat on the other.

"What's this?" he asked.

Peter already knew how Sean took his coffee—black in the morning—with milk and sugar the rest of the day—so he quickly filled a mug and handed it to him. "Breakfast. What do you think it is?"

"I don't usually eat breakfast."

Peter's stomach fell. "You don't? I'm sure it can keep for later. I can even eat it for dinner if you don't like it."

Sean shook his head. "That's not what I meant. I usually don't eat breakfast because I don't have time. I certainly don't have time to cook all of this. Thank you."

Peter licked his lips. He felt better now that he knew what Sean had been talking about, but not great yet. "It's the least I can do to thank you for all the help you're giving me."

Sean scowled. "I already told you to stop thanking me."

Peter crossed his arms over his chest. It was an argument they'd been having on and off since he'd arrived, and neither of them had won yet. "There's a *lot* to thank you for. You not only gave me a job but also a place to stay."

"Because you're my mate."

"It's not because of that. You agreed before we even met. You did it because you're a good person, and the least I can do is to thank you again and again."

Sean rubbed his face, then took a sip of coffee, smiling. "This is good." He frowned. "I won't allow you to distract me, though. You don't need to continue thanking me. It was awkward on the first day, and it's become even worse now. I know you're grateful. I don't understand why, but I get it. You don't need to continue thanking me. Please. I'm more than happy to do this for you."

Peter understood what Sean was saying. He realized that he'd been going overboard with the *thank yous*, and that he had to curb it. It was hard, though. He truly felt like if it hadn't been for Sean, he would be homeless right now, probably sleeping under a bridge or something like that.

He could have gone to his sister's, but he might not have managed to get there before his car broke down. She could have come to him, but she was working, and he doubted her bosses would have allowed her to come to the rescue.

No, Sean had saved Peter's life, even though he didn't seem to want to admit it. But Peter would do as he asked. He couldn't continue thanking him for the rest of their lives anyway, and since Sean knew how grateful he was, he might as well stop now.

He gestured at the table. "We should sit down."

Sean stared at Peter with narrow eyes for a moment, then nodded. "You're right. We should." He settled at the table, looking at the food again.

Peter wondered if he'd gone overboard. He hadn't just cooked pancakes. There was a tower of those, but there were also eggs, bacon, and even waffles. He hadn't been sure what Sean liked or ate for breakfast, and now, he realized he should have asked. It would have been the easiest way to go about this.

He rubbed the back of his neck and looked away. "I'm sorry if this is too much. I wasn't sure what you wanted to eat."

"I like everything you've put on the table, so that won't be a problem."

"There's a lot of it, though."

"And like you said, it can keep. Come on. You don't want to be late on your first day of work, do you?"

That made Peter smile. "Well, if I'm late, so are you, and I'm sure the boss won't have anything to say about it."

Sean barked out a laugh. "True that. But thank you, Peter. You didn't have to do all of this."

Peter had, though. He didn't know if Sean would understand, and he wasn't even sure it would be worth it trying to explain, so instead, he smiled and grabbed his fork.

"It's the least I could do," Peter repeated. He was still looking away from Sean, and Sean didn't like it. He also didn't like that Peter felt like he owed Sean something.

He didn't. He wasn't wrong when he said that Sean had agreed to help him even before they'd found out they were mates. Sean would have done a lot more for Emily's brother. He'd already told Peter they were family, even though they'd never met before, but Peter seemed to have a hard time understanding that.

So he'd gone overboard. It wasn't just breakfast, either. In the week since he'd arrived and since Sean had insisted that he take some time off work to recuperate from everything he'd gone through, Peter had cleaned the entire apartment from floor to ceiling—twice. Sean couldn't tell if he was one of those who cleaned when they were nervous or if he was trying to show Sean that he wouldn't regret taking him in, but he didn't like it either way. He wasn't a slob by any means, but now, the apartment felt more like one of the houses he flipped and tried to sell than a place in which they lived.

They would have to talk about it, but not now. Sean was touched by what Peter had been doing, by how hard he'd been trying to thank him, even though he shouldn't have. But no matter how many times Sean explained, Peter didn't get it, so he'd stopped trying. Maybe he would finally understand as time passed.

Sean could only hope.

He knew better than to push. Peter was very particular about some things, and apparently, especially so when it came to thanking him. He wanted Sean to know how thankful he was, and this was the way he did it. If he wanted to take care of breakfast and clean the house, that was fine with Sean. He truly was grateful for breakfast, since he didn't usually have time to eat, and while he could have done without the cleaning, there hadn't been a lot to do. If cleaning made Peter feel better and like he was home, Sean wasn't going to protest more than he already had.

They dug in, mostly in silence. Sean couldn't help but think about what was next for him and Peter. He didn't like having the kind of power he did over Peter, but he didn't know how to change that. He disliked being Peter's boss, even though Peter had taken it well. Peter had also insisted on paying rent, and Sean liked that even less.

It wouldn't be unheard of for two people who were together also to work together, so he was pretty sure he could get over that, at least until Peter found another job if that was what he wanted. Rent was different, though. Sean and his swan wanted to take care of their mate, and him paying to stay here wasn't working for them.

Sean had tried to make Peter understand that, but so far,

he hadn't managed. He'd be more than happy to help Peter find another job, but he didn't want Peter to move out. He knew Peter would as soon as he earned enough money, though. They were mates, and they were aware of it, but things were awkward between them. They weren't friends, and they weren't in love yet. They knew they were supposed to be together, but they hadn't managed to date. Peter had been overwhelmed, and Sean had work.

Now that their lives were stabilizing, though, Sean promised himself that he would do something. He wanted Peter to feel comfortable with him, to feel like he was home, and not to think about moving out. If he managed to do that, then he would be more than happy for Peter to find another job.

He'd known that Peter wouldn't work for him forever anyway. He wasn't a construction worker. He was an accountant, and even if he didn't love that job, it was what he knew, and apparently, how to do well.

"I'll start cleaning up," Peter said, getting to his feet.

Sean blinked at him. Peter had already finished eating, while Sean was still busy, having been lost in his thoughts. "I should be the one cleaning up. You cooked," he pointed out.

Peter's cheeks turned a light pink that was frankly adorable, and it made Sean want to kiss him. "Well, I haven't been doing anything for the past week. You've been working. I should be the one taking care of everything," Peter said.

"You're starting work today, though, and besides, it's not true that you haven't been doing anything. You cleaned the apartment. You settled into your room." Instead of Sean's bedroom, but that was okay.

Peter shrugged. "Again, I didn't have much to do, since you insisted on giving me a week of vacation."

Sean finished stuffing his face with the pancakes, pushed the last piece of bacon into his mouth, then got to his feet. "I'll help you," he muttered around his mouthful of food.

For some reason, that made Peter laugh. "All right. Thank you. You don't have to, but I appreciate it."

Sean watched him move for a moment. Then he started helping him. Together, they put away the leftovers, then rinsed and stacked the dishes into the dishwasher. They moved together as if they'd been doing it for years rather than a week, and it felt good. It felt *natural*, and that alone told Sean they would work well together.

He would do everything he could to have Peter in his life permanently. That was the one thing Sean was sure of, and what he wanted to work toward. He didn't know how he would make it happen yet, but he had time. Even though Peter was starting work today, it would take him a while to put away some money. Of course, he already had savings, so he might be able to afford an apartment sooner than Sean was comfortable with, especially in this small town.

The best way to go about this would be to talk to him, but Sean had avoided it. He didn't want to make Peter uncomfortable or push him in a direction he wasn't comfortable with, but he thought they should reassess what they both wanted from their relationship and talk again soon.

He didn't even have to think about it. He wanted Peter in his life, and possibly, in his home. For now, it was his apartment, and that was fine. They could find a house together in the future, once they were a couple. In the meantime, though, Sean didn't want Peter to move out. Well, if he moved out, he wanted it to be from his bedroom to Sean's.

Saying that would probably make Peter run away, though. He was skittish on the best of days, and while Sean understood why, he wanted that to change. He wanted Peter to be used to him, to view him like his mate, rather than a landlord.

"I'm going to finish getting ready," Peter said, already moving toward the door.

Sean caught his wrist. He acted on impulse, not thinking

about it, and he froze when Peter stopped moving and looked at him with wide eyes. He'd started this, though, so he might as well finish it.

He pulled Peter closer, then quickly kissed his forehead. "Thank you for breakfast," he murmured, still hovering close.

Peter blinked rapidly. "I told you that you didn't have to thank me, but I've been thanking you for a week, so I guess we're even."

Sean chuckled. "You didn't have to do this, and I'm grateful to have a full stomach."

"We should go get ready," Peter said, but he didn't move away, either.

They couldn't stay this way forever, though, so Sean kissed him again, then stepped toward the door. "You're right. We don't want to be late on your first day. It doesn't matter that I'm the boss—I'd be teased to no end."

"I hope it won't be a problem." Peter looked worried, and Sean didn't want him to be.

"It won't. I know the business is mine, but everyone who works with me is more like a family member. Don't worry too much, Peter. You'll fit in just fine." Just like he would fit in just fine with Sean's family, but Sean didn't mention them. It was way too soon for that.

Peter realized he was bouncing his knee while he and Sean were in the car. He stopped, pressing a hand against it.

He was nervous, and he suspected Sean knew that. It was no use trying to hide it, and he might as well stop. Besides, his knee seemed to have a life of its own and was bouncing again already.

He dug his fingers into his jeans. He had no idea what he was going to do today. He didn't know anything about construction work, and he wouldn't know where to start, even if he was given a hammer. He didn't have a choice, though. This was his job now, and he might as well wrap his mind around that and start thinking about whether or not he would end up hammering his own fingers or something like that. He wouldn't be surprised if they ended up in the emergency room, although he hoped that wouldn't be the case. It wouldn't exactly be the best way to start his new job.

"You don't have anything to be nervous about," Sean said without looking at Peter.

Peter was grateful for his mate's presence, but he also wished he could have gone to work on his own. His car was still with the mechanic, though, but he hoped to get it back soon. In the meantime, he and Sean were going to carpool, which could lead to embarrassing situations or conversations Peter didn't want to have.

He cleared his throat. "Wouldn't you be nervous if you were starting a new job?"

Sean chuckled. "I was always nervous when I worked with my father. He still does some work on the side, although he mostly builds furniture now. He's left construction work behind."

Sean hadn't talked a lot about his family. It was obvious he loved them, though—all of them, including his six brothers, and Peter had a hard time wrapping his mind around how many people that was. Sean had mentioned his father had built the construction business from the ground up. Sean had tried going to college, but it hadn't been for him, and he'd come back home. He'd started working with his father, who, once he knew that Sean could do it on his own, had decided to retire and focus on his true love—furniture making. Peter was curious and eager to see some of the pieces Sean's father and one of his brothers made, but so far, Sean hadn't talked about him meeting his family.

Peter wasn't sure what to think about that, either. Sean had already met the only family Peter wanted him to meet, which was his sister. Peter, on the other hand, had only met Sean. He didn't count Laurie, since they'd only had a short conversation. He knew about Sean's parents and his brothers, and he couldn't help but wonder if Sean was keeping him away from his family on purpose. With the way he spoke about his family, Peter suspected that they didn't usually stay away from each other for an entire week, which Sean had done since Peter had arrived. It made him wonder, but he told himself not to obsess over it. He didn't think that Sean was trying to hide him from his family on purpose, just that he wanted Peter to get used to his new life before he sicced them on him. It had to be that, or at least, Peter hoped so.

"But you're good at it now," he pointed out. Going back to talking about work felt safer.

"I'm good at it because I've been doing it for more than ten years. You can't expect to be as good as I am or as the people you'll be working with are. Don't worry too much, though. They were all beginners at one time, and they won't mind taking you under their wing. Besides, I explained that it was only a temporary job for you and that I was helping you get back on your feet. They don't expect too much from you."

Peter looked out the windshield. "I expect a lot from myself."

"And I understand that. But failing wouldn't have as many consequences as you think it would. It doesn't matter if you mess up, Peter. I won't fire you. I know you need this job, and I would never do something like that to you."

"Even if I ruined an entire house?"

"It would be tough for you to ruin an entire house, but if something like that happens, we'll talk and see what we can do."

"Are you doing this because were mates? I mean, the non-firing part?" Because things were bound to be awkward between them if he had to fire Peter.

"In part. In part, it's also because I want you to learn. I know you might decide you want to find another job, and it's perfectly fine if you do. But to me, you seem like the kind of person who wants to excel at everything you do. I can't say if you'll be a natural at construction, but I know you'll try, and that you'll try hard. That's good enough for me."

He wasn't wrong. Peter knew nothing about construction, but he'd promised himself he would try, and that even though he probably would never be perfect at it, he would do his best to make Sean proud. He was still planning on doing that, even though he was really fucking nervous.

Sean parked in front of a house, turned off the engine, and looked out the windshield. Peter sucked in a breath and reached for his door, but before he could open it, Sean grabbed his wrist.

It wasn't the first time he'd done it. It had happened in the kitchen earlier that morning, but Peter wasn't offended. He didn't mind Sean's hands on him. Actually, he *really* wouldn't mind if it happened more often. Still, he swallowed. He knew that whatever Sean had to say, it would have to do with the job, not with their relationship.

He turned toward Sean and forced himself to smile at him. "Yes?"

Sean looked serious when he gazed at Peter. "I don't want you to worry too much," he repeated. "This is just a job to tide you over. It's your first day, so no one expects anything from you. Just try to go along with everyone else and do what you're told. Be careful, because it's easy to get hurt when you're on a construction site. Do what we ask from you."

Peter sighed. He didn't like that people wouldn't expect anything from him. He always expected a lot of things from himself, and the thought of people already knowing he would be bad at this didn't sit well with him. He couldn't deny it was true, though. He didn't know where to start, and he would have to follow instructions. Hopefully, they would be clear enough that he wouldn't hurt himself, but it was anyone's guess at this point.

He nodded. "I'll do my best. I want to do well."

"I'm sure you'll be perfect," Sean murmured. Then, to Peter's surprise, he leaned even closer and gently kissed him on the lips this time.

They both lingered there, their lips brushing together. Peter closed his eyes and took a deep breath, inhaling Sean's scent without even thinking about it.

He felt better. He knew it was ridiculous, but being this close to his mate made him feel like he could do anything. Knowing that Sean didn't expect anything from him also helped. Whatever he managed to do today, Sean would be proud of him, and he should be proud of himself for not giving up and being ready to do anything it took to get back on his feet. It would have been easy to take advantage of Sean's kindness and the fact that they were mates, but Peter wasn't about to do that.

He'd had a lot of help, but he was pulling himself out of the disaster that was his life, and that was all that mattered.

"You can do this," Sean murmured. He kissed the tip of Peter's nose, winked at him, and finally leaned back and left the truck.

Peter stared at him for a moment. He had to leave the truck, too, even though it felt like a safe place. Instead of staying where he was and hiding from the world, he took a deep breath, then followed Sean.

He looked up at the house. He felt a little dazed, possibly because of the kiss, more probably because of what was about to happen. But it wasn't the first time he'd had a first day on a job, and he knew he could do it.

He felt better. He knew that whatever happened, as long as

he didn't burn the house down, Sean would be happy with the results. It helped to know that, and he straightened his shoulders, knowing he could do this. He could make Sean proud, and himself, too.

Sean knew Peter was still nervous when they walked into the house they were renovating, and especially so when he was faced by the five members of Sean's team, who were huddled in the entrance talking. Still, Peter did his best not to let it show, and Sean was proud of him.

"Hey, boss," Tyler said. "We weren't sure you were going to get out of the truck. I thought you'd rather go home and continue what you were doing out there," he teased as he wiggled his eyebrows.

Peter's cheeks looked like they went up in flames, and Sean playfully glared at Tyler. "None of your business."

"I think it *is* our business," Dylan said. He was leaning against the wall with his arms crossed over his chest. He didn't look angry or anything like that, though. If anything, he was smiling, which made it obvious that he was teasing, too.

Sean threw his hands up in the air. "Don't you have anything to do? We're here to work, not to make fun of me."

Maddie smiled. "But it's so much fun to tease you. Why don't you introduce us?"

Sean put a hand on the small of Peter's back and gently pushed him forward. "Everyone, this is Peter. And yes, the two of us are mates, so you can shut it," he declared.

Peter stared at him with wide eyes, and Sean smiled. "We're all shifters here. The owners aren't, so you have to be careful about what you say around them, but they're not supposed to come around until this afternoon. You can be yourself with the rest of the crew, though."

Peter slowly nodded, then turned his attention back to the crew. "As you probably already know, I'm Peter, and yes, I'm his mate."

Sean had never been so grateful for the people he'd hired than when they came closer and offered Peter their hands. They lined up, something Sean found hilarious, but he was grateful for their support.

"That's Maddie," he said, going in order as Peter shook their hands. "She usually takes care of the yards and pools, things like that, but she pitches in if we need help anywhere else. Don't let her appearance fool you—she can probably carry more weight then you can." She was a petite blonde, and men especially always underestimated her.

Peter laughed, and it was good to hear him like this. He was still nervous, probably, but maybe he was starting to realize that these people weren't going to eat him and that he could be himself with them. Sean had told them what had happened to Peter, and he'd already mentioned the fact that they were together. They knew what to expect, and that this wasn't going to be Peter's job forever. He was only here until he got his feet under him, and that was fine with them. It was how most of them had started, and while they hadn't left, Sean wouldn't be surprised if at least a few of them were planning to in the future. Hopefully, not anytime soon, but he would deal with it if he had to. He wanted his people to be happy, even if it wasn't from working for him.

"That's Jude, the quiet one. He takes care of the design, and he's an architect. He's the one who starts the work, and we just follow his orders," Sean said. "Tyler, the loudmouth, is our electric guy. Dylan takes care of the plumbing, and the last one is Kincaid, who you can call King because he has a big head. He takes care of the walls, painting, all of that stuff."

Peter finished shaking hands, then turned to Sean. "What about you? What do *you* take care of?"

Tyler barked a laugh. "Yes, why don't you tell him? Because I'm still trying to figure that out."

Sean playfully glared at him. "Get to work."

Tyler saluted him, but he didn't leave, and Sean turned to Peter. "I take care of everything wood. I took that from my dad, I guess. I don't make furniture, but railings, porches, kitchen cabinets, things like that. Even the structure around which we build houses. If you have something to do that involves wood, come to me, and I'll help you."

Peter looked around. The house wasn't a mess, because Sean wanted everyone on his crew to be neat, but it was very much under construction. "What am I supposed to do? I don't know how to do anything you just mentioned."

Before Sean could say anything, Kincaid slapped Peter on the shoulder, making him stumble. "Don't worry too much. You'll get used to it, and even though you can't do anything right now, you'll learn. In the meantime, you just help any of us who needs another set of hands. Sometimes, it's useful to have someone who can move around and help whoever's in need."

"I thought Maddie did that," Peter said, looking at Kincaid as if he didn't believe him.

"I do, but this house has a yard, and I have to work on that," Maddie said. "If you want, you can start with me. We'll go outside, and I'll explain what I had in mind."

Peter looked at Sean, and Sean nodded. "Go with her. It's not a problem. I expect you to familiarize yourself with the work and the house today. Just get your bearings, okay? And if you need anything, you can come to find me or anyone else in the crew. They won't mind."

He watched Peter disappear outside with Maddie, then turned to the other four. "And you, get to work. If Peter comes to you and wants to learn, I'd appreciate it if you helped him, but it's not an obligation."

"Of course we'll teach him," Jude said quietly. "He's your mate, and even if he doesn't stay with us forever, he'll still be a part of our lives. I'm happy for you, Sean. We all are."

That made Sean feel better and warm inside. "Good. And thank you. Now, get to work."

Jude probably wouldn't be staying the entire day. He worked in an office rather than in the houses the way everyone else did, but he was still around most days.

Sean had work to do, too, but before he could get to it, his phone rang. He rolled his eyes when he saw his mother's name flash on the screen. He knew if he didn't answer, she would call again and again until he did. She was curious about Peter, and she wanted Sean to bring him around. She'd given him an entire week to get used to this new life and his new job, and she probably thought it was more than enough.

Sean wasn't too sure about that, but he did know that he should answer. "What's up?" he asked as he did so.

"You know why I'm calling, so don't try that with me, Sean. You're not too old for me to spank you."

Sean laughed. His mom had never raised a hand to him or any of his brothers, and she'd certainly never spanked them. "Sure. What did you need, Mom?"

"When are you bringing Peter to dinner?"

Sean sighed. He hadn't told his mom yet that Peter was his mate. He knew that when he did, she would *demand* to meet him right away, and he'd wanted to give Peter time to get comfortable, and hopefully, for them to be a couple. He supposed he might as well tell her now, though. That way she wouldn't swamp him and Peter with hugs and kisses.

He cleared his throat and looked around, but he was alone. "He's still uncomfortable, and he started work today. Maybe at the end of the week?"

"You can't bring him sooner?"

"I don't know, Mom. But I don't want you to scare him off.

He's my mate."

There was a moment of silence, and Sean was grateful that his mom wasn't the screeching kind. "Oh, Sean. I'm so happy for you," she said, her voice softer.

"I'm happy, too. I like him, Mom. That's why I don't want to scare him off. I know you mean well, but he's overwhelmed right now. He lost everything, and even though he's slowly working to replace it, it's still a lot. Plus, there's me to deal with, and I know I'm not easy."

His mom guffawed. "I won't touch *that* declaration with a ten feet pole, but you're right. We can be overwhelming, and it's probably not the best idea to add that to him in his situation. Just mention it to him, all right? Now that I know he's your mate, I want to meet him even more. I want to see you happy."

"I already am. You don't have to worry about that. We're working things out, but it's going to be a slow process."

"That's okay. Just let me know what's going on, okay?"

"I promise."

He hoped it was a promise he would be able to keep. He wanted him and Peter to be together before he introduced him to his family, but it might not happen, and that was okay. Sean had promised he wouldn't push, and he was planning on keeping that promise. Whatever time Peter needed from Sean, he would get it.

Chapter Four

They'd settled into a routine that was now familiar to Peter, and probably to Sean, too. It was a bit startling, but Peter couldn't say he regretted it. If anything, it made him feel better, more at peace. Or maybe it was because he was settling in well. He didn't know why he felt that way, but he wasn't going to protest or try to find a problem where there wasn't one.

He'd been applying for jobs, but so far, he hadn't gotten any answers. That was okay, though. He was working for Sean, and even though he was a bit of a klutz when it came to construction—and he should have expected it—it worked well enough. He was at the beck and call of everyone else, and even though he hadn't been sure about it, it was the best thing he could do. That way, they were free to focus on the work, and he didn't feel like he was about to make the house explode or something just as bad. Sean had said that as long as Peter was okay with whatever he was doing and comfortable, he could do whatever he wanted, so that was what Peter was doing at work.

But he wasn't at work, and he had to call his sister.

She was worried about him. They hadn't talked in a week, and she knew how anxious he was about the job, living with Sean, and everything else. He'd texted her, but he knew that wouldn't be enough. He and Emily were close, and that would never change. He didn't want to push her away, so it was time to tell her what was going on. Thankfully, Peter only had good things to say.

"I still can't believe you're mates," Emily said when she

answered.

Peter couldn't help but smile. "Not even a hello?"

"Yes, hello. How are you and Sean doing?"

"I thought you would want to know about my job. Maybe about how apartment hunting is going."

There was a pause, and it made Peter realize what he'd said. He was playing around, but Emily would take it seriously, and he wasn't looking forward to that conversation.

"You're thinking of moving out?" she asked.

Peter sighed and leaned back against the headboard of his bed. He'd just showered, and his hair was still damp. He could hear Sean moving around in the kitchen. He didn't know what Sean was cooking — Sean had admitted he wasn't a great cook — but they would eat, and that was what mattered. They were both starving after a day of work.

"In part," he admitted.

"Why? Sean's your mate. Why would you want to move out?"

"Because even though he's my mate, he didn't ask me to move in with him because of that. He was trying to help me, to help *you*, and I don't know if that's the best start for a relationship." Right now, Sean was everything in Peter's life. He was the one who gave him a roof over his head, who put food in his stomach, and gave him a job. Peter was entirely dependent on him, and he didn't like it. He'd never been dependent on anyone, not after he'd graduated from high school, and he hadn't thought it would happen again. He was relieved he didn't have to go back to his parents, but he didn't know if this was much better. Yes, Sean was his mate, and he didn't care that Peter depended on him, but Peter was uncomfortable.

Emily sighed. "Okay, I get it. You want to stand on your own two feet, and that's fine. It doesn't mean you have to move out, though."

"It should. I need to get my own place and a new job. I need not to depend on him anymore." Because if he did, how could he be sure that what he felt for Sean was genuine?

"You could just pay rent. That's how couples work, Peter. I know you don't usually think that way, but Sean doesn't care that you depend on him. He'll only care that *you* care about it, and I think that's great."

"Has he told you anything?" That was one problem of dating your sister's best friend. Peter suspected they talked about him behind his back, and he was both terrified of those conversations and happy that Sean had someone to talk to.

"A bit. He's happy, Peter. I've never heard him so happy."

"And you don't want me to fuck things up."

She chuckled. "I don't, no. And I think you'll work things out. You're overthinking this, but then, you're an overthinker. I understand that you want to be independent, and I'm sure Sean will, too, but it doesn't mean you have to leave him behind to make it happen. You can stand on your own independently, find a job that isn't related to him, and start paying rent and bills. Make the apartment a place you share, not one that's just Sean's."

"It's in his name, though," Peter pointed out, even though his protest wasn't as strong as it should have been.

"Then you two should look for a house together. That way, both your names will be on the contract."

"Is that something Sean wants to do?"

Emily hesitated. "It's something he's always talked about, yes. I probably shouldn't be telling you this, but there's a reason he lives in a small apartment even though he owns a construction company. He was waiting for his mate to find a house they both loved and to fix it up the way they both wanted. Well, the way *you* both want. You should talk to him about that, though. But please, don't obsess over being independent. Don't try to be an island. I know that after what happened with our parents, you don't want to depend on anyone, but being in a relationship also means that. It's good to be independent, but it's also good to know that you have someone you can rely on when you need it. He won't hurt you, Peter. He's my best friend, but you're my brother. I would tell you if I thought it was a bad idea."

Peter closed his eyes. She wasn't wrong, and she did know Sean better than he did.

But he was starting to get to know his mate, and he liked what he was finding out. Sean was a good man, a joyful one, a caring one. He didn't seem to have a lot of friends, or if he did, Peter hadn't met many of them, but Sean loved his family, and it was huge. He had six brothers, and Peter suspected he'd been keeping them away while he was here. He hoped it was only to give him time to get used to everything, but he knew that wouldn't last forever. He was going to have to meet Sean's parents and his brothers sooner or later.

Then there was the people who worked for Sean. He didn't act as if he was the boss, but rather, as if they all worked together. They talked things out, and he didn't order anyone around.

And finally, there was Peter. The two of them worked well together, and they were good at sharing the apartment. Peter felt like he belonged here, and even though Sean hadn't said anything, Peter suspected he felt the same way.

So why was he thinking about moving out? Emily wasn't wrong. It was good to have someone Peter knew would always be there for him, someone he could rely on when he needed it. Sean had been that person, and he always would be since they were mates. Besides, how did couples work? They shared a home, and they both paid for the necessities. Surely, Peter and Sean could do the same?

"I have to go," Peter said, opening his eyes.

"You'll talk to him?"

"I don't know. But he's waiting for me to eat dinner, and I don't want to disappoint him." He never wanted to disappoint Sean.

"Just think about it for a bit. I know Sean won't push you to make decisions. It's not the kind of person he is. I want you two to be happy, and I know you'll be perfect together, as long as you can get over your fear of being in a relationship."

Peter froze. "I'm not afraid of relationships."

He could hear the soft smile in Emily's voice when she answered, "A bit. I think you're afraid that you're going to lose your boyfriend, just like you lost our parents. They should have been there for you, but instead, they kicked you out. Now you're afraid to trust. You can trust Sean, though. I promise you that."

Peter wanted to believe her. He did believe her. She wasn't wrong when she said that he was afraid. His parents should have shielded him from the world and accepted him the way he was, and they hadn't.

Could he trust Sean to do it instead?

Something was different. Sean didn't know what it was, but he wanted to find out. He'd felt it since Peter had come back from his shower, and Sean couldn't help trying to read him.

Peter was more confident. Sean thought it was because he was finally getting back on his feet, and he liked what he saw. He liked it when Peter did what he wanted without asking, as if he belonged here. He noticed Sean checking the stove—the water in the pot wasn't heating for some reason—and hip-checked him as he took a look.

So Sean was a bit of a disaster in the kitchen. Peter didn't seem to mind coming to the rescue and finding out what was wrong, which was that he'd forgotten to turn the gas on under the pot of water.

Sean was ashamed for all of two seconds. Then he started laughing. Peter laughed with him, and after that, they worked on cooking dinner together. It wasn't anything complicated, just spaghetti and meat sauce, but they worked in the small kitchen as if they'd been doing it for decades.

They fit together perfectly.

Sean had known this would happen. They wouldn't be mates if they weren't perfect for each other, or maybe they wouldn't be perfect for each other if they weren't mates. He didn't know which way things went, and it didn't matter. The only thing that did was that he and Peter were working things out, even though Sean wasn't sure where they stood just yet.

The past week had been interesting. After the first few casual kisses they'd exchanged when Sean had been reassuring Peter, they'd started kissing more often. They hadn't made out yet, but there was always a small touch on Sean's arm, on the small of Peter's back, light kisses exchanged in the evening while they watched TV on the couch.

They touched as if it was something they were used to doing, and Sean wanted more. It took his breath away every time Peter reached for him, and it was all it took not to reach back for Peter, to pull him in his lap and kiss him senseless. That was what he and his swan wanted to do, but Sean didn't want to spook Peter. The worst thing that could happen was Peter getting scared and deciding to leave.

Sean knew Peter was looking for a new job, and he hadn't said anything about it. He wanted Peter to be comfortable, to like what he did. And even though Peter didn't hate working with Sean and the others, Sean could tell it wasn't his thing. That was okay. He didn't want it to be Peter's thing. He *did* want Peter to stay with him, though, and possibly, to move from the guest room to Sean's bedroom.

Everything would come in time, and Sean had to focus on draining the pasta.

They kept looking at each other as they sat at the small table. To Sean's surprise, Peter hooked his legs around his, pulling his foot closer. They ate like that, their legs tangled together, peeking at each other like teenagers on their first date. Peter was flustered, and it made Sean smile until he couldn't stop.

He liked this. It felt like they were on a date, even though they weren't. They really should talk about it, but he was afraid to break the moment, to shatter the fragile hope he had that Peter was accepting him as his mate. He thought that had been happening for a while, but he wouldn't know for sure until he asked, and it was terrifying.

Putting himself out there like that was scary. But Peter was Sean's mate, and if Sean couldn't talk to him of all people, who could he talk to?

"Go sit on the couch," Peter said after dinner. "I'll clean up."

"You don't have to." They'd taken the habit of dividing the chores. If one of them cooked, the other cleaned up. Sean wanted Peter close tonight, though, and he wouldn't mind cleaning up.

Peter shook his head. "It's the rule. You cooked, so I'll clean."

"I wouldn't even have cooked if you hadn't realized that I hadn't turned the heat on under the pot. Come on. Let me help you. That way, we'll be done sooner, and we can sit on the couch and watch something."

Peter hesitated, but Sean knew what he wanted. Peter loved spending time on the couch, watching TV, and casually chatting. Every evening, they sat closer to each other, and Sean couldn't help but wonder if eventually Peter would end up in his lap, or the other way around.

He hoped so. He hoped that and many other things would happen.

"Fine. Since you're offering, I won't argue," Peter finally said, and Sean shot to his feet.

Peter laughed, and they got to work. They were silent once again, and Sean realized that it wasn't the same as his other relationships. Back then, he'd always tried to fill the silence because it wasn't comfortable, and it felt like he didn't have anything to say to the guy he was dating.

It was different with Peter. Sean had a lot of things to say. He wanted to tell Peter he loved him. He wanted to tell him that he wanted to spend the rest of his life with him. All of those words hung in the air between them, and he knew he didn't need to say them out loud for Peter to know them. It made the silence easier to deal with, lighter, as if it was something normal in their relationship. And maybe it would be. They might be mates, but they still needed to work on the relationship, and Sean thought they were doing a good job. He couldn't wait to see what happened in the next few years, but more importantly, in the next two *hours*.

He had a feeling something had changed tonight, and he wanted to find out what it was. He sat on the couch once they were done cleaning the kitchen and held his breath. Peter was still turning the lights off, so he was the one who would have to choose where to sit. He'd always sat on the couch next to Sean, but he'd started on the other side of the couch, then had inched closer and closer to Sean every day. There was still some space between them, but to Sean's delight, when Peter came in, he sat right next to him. Sean's heart raced as he stretched his arm out, hooking it around Peter's shoulders. He said there, tense, ready to take his arm away if it made Peter uncomfortable, but Peter just tilted his head to look at Sean and smiled at him.

They were doing this. There were cuddling on the couch, and Sean couldn't have been happier.

He turned the TV on, tuning to a movie he didn't

recognize, mostly because he couldn't stop looking at Peter. Peter snuggled even closer, pressing his cheek against Sean's chest and sighing happily as he did so.

Sean couldn't resist. "What do you want?" he asked, his voice slightly hoarse.

Peter tensed only to relax again. He tilted his head so they could look each other in the eyes, then, he wound one of his arms around Sean's waist.

"What do you mean?" Peter asked.

Sean swallowed. He'd promised himself he wouldn't push, but it was what he was doing, or maybe not. It had been two weeks. He needed an answer, at least a partial one. "I don't want to resist you, Peter. I've been doing that for two weeks, and I don't want to do it anymore," he murmured.

He dropped the remote control and dug his hand into Peter's hair. "I want you. I want us to share a bed. I want us to kiss and to be together as a couple. We've been inching toward that, but it's not enough, not anymore." He swallowed. "Unless it's a problem for you. I promise that I can wait as long as you need me to. I just want some answers."

Peter bit his lower lip. Sean could tell he was making a decision, and he held his breath. It came out in a whoosh when Peter reached up and kissed him.

This kiss wasn't one of the light ones they'd been exchanging until now. Peter's tongue prodded at Sean's lips until he opened them. Then Peter moved, straddling Sean's thighs and wrapping his arms around Sean's neck, holding him close as Peter kissed him senseless the way Sean had wanted to do to him. There was nothing Sean could do except wrap his own arms around Peter's waist and kiss him back.

He had to make sure, though. The kiss didn't tell him what Peter wanted, not in words. "What do you want?" he asked again between two kisses, while Peter was nuzzling his neck.

"I thought it was obvious," Peter murmured. He

straightened and looked right at Sean. "I want you. You're my knight in shining armor, and I've wanted you since the beginning. I was afraid to give you my heart, but I know it's useless because you already have it. You've had it since day one, and the only thing I can hope for is that you won't break it."

Peter was all over the place, but for the first time in weeks, he was convinced of what he was doing. He'd been afraid when he'd had to leave everything behind, but Sean had been there to catch him. He would always be there to catch him, and that helped. Peter didn't like being dependent on anyone, not even Sean, but Emily was right. If he couldn't be dependent on his mate, then he would forever have to be on his own, and that wasn't how life worked. Everyone needed someone else sometimes, and for Peter, that someone else was Sean.

So he kissed Sean. He wanted more, just like Sean did. He didn't know what yet, but he supposed he was about to find out.

Sean cupped one of Peter's cheeks, stopping him from leaning down and kissing him again. "I'm not a knight in shining armor," he murmured.

"You feel like it. You saved me when I was alone in the world, and I didn't have a home or anything else."

"You weren't alone. You always have Emily."

"But it's not the same. Even though she wanted to help, she couldn't. You, on the other hand, offered all of this to someone you didn't know. You stepped up and saved me, just like a knight." Peter meant it. He didn't understand how Sean could be so nice, so gentle with someone he didn't know.

He'd been generous, offering Peter a bedroom and a job only on the basis that he was Emily's brother. What if Peter had been an asshole? What if he'd made Sean's life hell? Peter suspected Sean would still have stuck to his end of the deal, helping him until he was back on his feet. Peter *wasn't* an asshole, but still. Knowing that Sean was ready to do something like that made Peter's heart soften—as if it needed to soften more when it came to Sean.

Peter wasn't lying when he said he'd wanted this since the first day. Hell, he'd been falling in love with Sean since then. The way Sean took care of him and everyone else, the way he'd given him space even though he clearly hadn't wanted to, all of that made Sean the perfect man for Peter. Peter didn't know what would happen in the future, but he did know one thing—he would always have Sean. He would always be with him, but that wasn't something he was willing to think about right now. It was too big, too intimidating.

No, the only thing he wanted to think about at the moment was him and Sean, and hopefully, Sean's bed.

They should have a conversation first. Peter realized Sean wouldn't soften until he knew what was going on. He was so afraid of hurting Peter and doing something Peter would regret that he seemed to be frozen in indecision.

Peter leaned down and kissed Sean's cheek. "Thank you for worrying about me and wanting to be sure I'm okay. But I am, Sean. I've been thinking about this since the beginning, and I wanted it for just as long."

"But something changed." Sean's hands tightened on Peter's hips, as if he was afraid Peter was going to run away instead of answering.

"I talked with Emily, and she made me see why I was holding back. I was afraid. The two people who should have had my back, who should have always been there for me and should have shielded my heart, threw it away. My parents didn't accept me when I came out to them, even though they should have. I've been afraid of loving anyone else since then, including you. I was afraid of letting you in, but Emily made me see that. She made me understand why I was so scared, and I know that if I don't take this step, I never will. And I *want* to take it. I don't want to push you away anymore. I want you in my life, Sean."

Sean stroked a hand up and down Peter's back. "And you're okay with me giving you a job and my guest room?"

"I'm already trying to find another job. No offense, because I actually like working with you, but it's not my thing. As for the guest room, well, as soon as I start earning enough money, I want to pay rent, or at the very least, to help you with the bills. Please. I need to do it." He held his breath.

He wasn't surprised when Sean nodded and said, "Of course. Anything to make you feel comfortable. That's what was holding you back?"

Peter sighed. "I didn't want to owe you anything. I thought you could use it against me, and you can. But you won't, because you're not that kind of person."

"I could be. We haven't known each other long."

"We haven't, no. But it's long enough for me to know this is the right thing to do, at least for me."

Sean stared at Peter for a while, then nodded. "It is for me, too. I want you, Peter. I thought I would have to wait a long time, but I'm happy I won't. I never want you to feel pushed into anything, though. We can stop anytime. We can just kiss the rest of the night. I don't expect anything from you apart from telling me whether or not you're comfortable and what you want."

Peter swallowed. "I'll tell you what I want, then. I want you to take me to bed. I want you to kiss me, to strip me, to make love to me. I don't care how we do that or who does what. I just want to be one with you." He yearned for it, but he didn't want to seem too eager, although he doubted that would be a problem when it came to Sean. He seemed just as eager as Peter.

Peter squeaked when Sean suddenly got to his feet, still

holding him. He had to wrap himself around his mate, hanging on for dear life. He hadn't realized Sean could do something like that, although it made sense. Sean worked construction, and his muscles had muscles. They were all hard and moving under Peter's hands. Peter ran his palms over them, doing his best to keep his balance as Sean walked both of them to the bedroom.

Sean's bedroom.

Peter had been in there before to leave baskets of clean laundry on Sean's bed. This time was different, though, and he saw it differently. If everything went well, this was where Peter would be sleeping from now on. It felt good to know that he still had the guest bedroom if he needed space, but he suspected he wouldn't. Now that he'd admitted to himself and to Sean that he wanted Sean and that he'd opened himself up to his mate, it felt like there was no going back.

Sean delicately put Peter down on the bed. Peter knew he had to go, but it was hard. He wanted to keep Sean there, pressed against him, to truly become one with him. He didn't know if that was what they were going to do tonight, but either way, it felt like whatever happened, they would wake up changed tomorrow.

They were mates, and this was the first step in their life together.

Sean took off his t-shirt, then reached for his jeans. He looked down at Peter, who was staring at him. Peter hadn't been moving, and Sean arched a brow at him.

Peter reached for his t-shirt, too, but Sean stopped him. "I want to do that," he said, a hand on Peter's wrist.

Peter dropped his hands to the mattress. "I'm at your disposal."

And he was. He trusted Sean to keep him safe and happy.

Sean quickly stripped, and Peter mourned the fact that he hadn't been able to do it or to enjoy the moment. Sean moved quickly and efficiently, clearly ready for more, and Peter knew they would have other opportunities to take their time.

He wasn't in as much as a hurry as Sean, but he couldn't deny that he was hard and that he wanted Sean in a way he'd never wanted anyone else. He *had* to see if this would be as good as he'd dreamed it would be.

Probably better, now that he thought about it. He might just die tonight, but he would die in the best of ways.

Once Sean was naked, he turned his attention to Peter. His gaze was intense, and Peter couldn't help but grin. He sat up, because there was no other way for Sean to help him out of his t-shirt, and together, they worked on getting Peter naked. Sean grunted a few times, clearly unhappy that Peter was working, too, but Peter ignored him.

Sean hadn't taken his time, and neither would Peter. He wanted this as much as Sean did, and he didn't see a reason to waste time, not when one of them was already naked and when it was their first time. Plus, he wanted to feel every-thing.

Sean pushed him on his back, then hovered over him, look-ing down with heat in his eyes. "What do you want? How do you want to do this?"

Peter didn't care, but he knew Sean wanted an answer. The first thing that came to mind was that he wanted everything, but he suspected he wasn't quite ready for it. He was giving Sean his heart, his life, his everything, but him realizing they had time to do all of it made him feel better and more settled.

He wasn't going anywhere. Even when he found a job, he would stay here with Sean. They had the rest of their lives, and he didn't want to rush, not when it came to this.

So he wrapped himself around Sean, pulling him down on top of him. Sean's skin was warm, his body hard, but he still settled between Peter's legs as if he belonged there.

And he did.

Sean wanted to take care of Peter. He could think of nothing better to do right now, and he knew Peter needed it. Peter tried to be strong, and now that he'd explained why, it made sense. Sean had known that Peter's parents hadn't been accepting, and now that Peter was his, he wanted to find them and yell at them for abandoning their child. He couldn't, though. He *wouldn't*. Peter had left them behind as part of his old life, while Sean was part of the new one. That was what Sean should focus on—that, and Peter.

Peter, who was strong yet vulnerable. Peter, who was stretched under him, entirely naked, waiting for him to do *something*. He'd curled himself around Sean, but that was it. He wasn't demanding, wasn't asking. He was just waiting, and Sean yearned to give him everything he'd ever wished for.

Peter hadn't said anything about fucking, and besides, it wasn't what they were doing. They were making love, and since Sean wasn't willing to push too hard, he decided to stick with things that didn't involve condoms. Besides, they needed to have a conversation about that. He never wanted Peter to do anything he wasn't ready for or willing to do, especially when it came to sex. He wanted both of them to enjoy themselves, so instead of reaching for the lube in his nightstand, he kissed Peter again.

Peter moaned and kissed him back. He reacted to Sean's touch like a dream, and Sean couldn't stop himself from touching every inch of his body he could find.

Peter's skin was smooth and sprinkled with hair. His body was softer than Sean's, and Sean loved it. He liked the way Peter's stomach trembled when Sean ran a hand down his side and the way he pushed up when Sean found his cock. Sean didn't give him what he wanted, though, not yet. He wanted to drive Peter crazy, to make him see how much he cared for him and what he wanted to give him, so he set out to do just that. He kissed a path down Peter's neck, lingering at his nipples, giving them the attention that they deserved. He licked, sucked, kissed, and even bit down a few times, making Peter writhe under him. Peter's hands were buried into Sean's hair, and from the pulling and pushing, Sean could tell what Peter wanted him to focus on.

He probably would have been able to tell even without that guidance. Peter's hips strained upward, his cock calling for Sean. Sean licked his lips when he came face to face with it, but instead of taking him into his mouth, he looked up. Peter was looking down at him with hooded eyes, waiting. They stared at each other for a moment, then, instead of sucking Peter off, Sean kissed his inner thigh.

Peter huffed and pressed his head back against the pillow. "You're driving me crazy," he whispered, gently pulling on Sean's hair.

"That's not what I was trying to do. I just wanted to show you how much I care about you. Driving you crazy is a bonus."

"You don't have to. I already know you care about me."

He probably did. Sean wasn't exactly discreet when it came to that kind of thing. But he could tell that Peter was both strong and fragile, and he wanted to protect him and help him hold himself up. He wanted to be part of the life Peter was rebuilding without taking over.

Peter was fiercely independent. He'd had to be, especially after his parents had kicked him out of their lives. He'd had Emily, but this was different.

Sean wanted Peter to see that he didn't have to be alone anymore. Sean would never take the place of Peter's parents or his sister, but there *was* a place for him in Peter's life. He fit there perfectly, being Peter's rock, the one person he could lean on if something happened. Peter would never be alone again. Even if something happened between him and Sean, he would always have Sean's family. They might not have met him yet, but Sean was sure of that. It was just the way they were. They wouldn't agree to anything less.

Neither would Sean. He wanted Peter not to be alone. He wanted to be part of his life, but he also wanted Peter to realize that he could rely on other people. He didn't have to stand strong all the time.

The best way to make him understand that was to take care of him, even in bed, maybe especially so. It seemed to be the one place in which Peter was more comfortable expressing what he wanted and opening up, and Sean wanted to take advantage of it.

He looked at Peter's cock, but once again, he avoided it. Instead of touching it, he went down Peter's legs, kissing them, too. He licked behind Peter's knees, smiling when he realized that Peter was ticklish when it came to his feet. He didn't even want Sean to touch them, which was okay. Sean still kissed the top of both, but he didn't linger on them. Instead, he moved upward again.

"I hope you're about to give me what I want," Peter muttered.

"Always. You never have to ask."

Peter rolled his eyes. "You couldn't have told me that sooner? Come on, Sean. Come up here."

Sean blinked. "You don't want me to suck you?"

"I do, more than anything. I'm pretty sure I'll blow after five seconds, though. I need you, Sean. I need you on top of me, holding me close. I *want* you here."

Sean was relieved. He'd been teasing Peter, but at the same time, he was teasing himself, too. His cock felt like it was about to explode, so he obeyed Peter's order, pressing their bodies together. Just like before, Peter wrapped himself around him, holding him close, and Sean knew that this time, he wouldn't let him go.

That was perfectly fine with him. If he had his way, he would *never* let Peter go.

Sean wiggled until his cock settled in the groove between Peter's thigh and his groin. The wiggling made Peter laugh, and Sean smiled. He loved sex, but he loved sex with Peter even more. They were having fun as they discovered each other's bodies and what they liked and didn't like, and it was perfect. Sex didn't have to be serious. After all, there was nothing serious about sex. People were naked, usually sweating and wet with saliva and other bodily fluids. They flopped together on a bed until they finally reached pleasure.

What was serious about that?

He kissed Peter again, and Peter sighed happily. He relaxed, and together, they moved, chasing their pleasure, but also the completion that would bring them together. It wasn't just sex. It wasn't just an orgasm. It was so much more, yet it wasn't.

Sean screwed his eyes shut as he felt the pleasure mounting. He could tell Peter was right behind him, and he had to feel it. He held his hips back, pushing his hand between them, curling his fingers around Peter's cock.

Peter cried out. Sean grinned against the skin of his mate's neck, then pulled on his cock. Peter tried to push them even closer together, but with Sean's arm between them, it was impossible.

Peter trembled as he came. He cried out Sean's name, holding on to him. He screwed his eyes shut and threw his head back, looking beautiful. Sean was gentle as he guided him through the pleasure, but as soon as he was done and went all floppy and relaxed in Sean's arms, Sean moved his hand to his own cock. He was so close already that it only took a few pulls until he added his release to Peter's. Then he moved to the side to allow Peter to breathe, but Peter would have none of that.

He threw his arms and legs back around Sean, and they both rolled until they were on their sides, staring at each other. They were pressed together, and Sean kissed Peter again, smiling.

"Thank you," Peter murmured.

"I don't know what you're thanking me for, but you're welcome."

Peter laughed. "I didn't expect this to happen, but I'm happy it did."

So was Sean. He wanted to ask what was next for them, but he knew Peter was still unsure of himself and of the way his life was going. Sean wanted to help, but he decided that tonight, they should focus on the pleasure of being with each other.

The future would be there soon enough, and they would deal with it when it came.

CHAPTER FIVE

Peter couldn't remember the last time he'd been so happy. It had been a while, if he was honest with himself. When he lived in the city, he'd had an apartment and a good job, but he hadn't been this happy. He found it ironic that now that he had neither of those things, he was happier than ever.

He knew it had a lot—if not everything—to do with Sean. Now that they'd finally broken the barrier between them, they were a couple, and Peter had never thought he would have this. He was incredibly happy, and he wanted more, so much more. He didn't know what exactly, but he did know that he wasn't planning on going anywhere, not anymore.

Sean had told him he didn't expect him to find another apartment, and Peter had agreed, as long as he could help pay the bills. It had been obvious Sean wasn't happy with that, but he'd agreed. He understood that Peter needed to contribute and know he could survive on his own if something happened.

Peter was grateful. He didn't know what he would have done if Sean hadn't understood and if he'd pushed for Peter to stay with him without paying his way. That wasn't the case, though, and Peter couldn't wait to find a new job so they could start the life they would have together.

And talking about a new job, he'd just gotten an email from one of the jobs he'd applied for in Boston, and he wasn't quite sure what to do with it. They were asking for an online interview since he'd told them he wasn't in Boston anymore, and he didn't know whether or not he should accept.

Sean was in the shower, and Peter was grateful. He knew this wouldn't go down well with Sean, not because Sean didn't want him to find another job that made him happier than the one, he had with his company, but because it was so far. It had taken Peter hours to get here by car that first day, and the same would be true if he had to go back. There was no way for them to make it work, not with that distance. They could try having a long-distance relationship, but Peter wasn't sure he wanted that.

That left him with a dilemma. Should he turn the interview down? Getting the job would mean that he had to move back and leave Sean behind. He didn't want that, but he also didn't want to ruin his possibilities of having a job he found more appealing than hammering nails the entire day.

On the other hand, he didn't want to leave town. He didn't want to leave *Sean*, and he was ready to continue working with him if that was what it took to stay with him. He didn't know if he could decline the interview, though.

In short, he didn't know what he wanted. Apart from Sean, of course, but that wouldn't happen if he chose the job.

In the end, he quickly answered, agreeing to an interview. He had no idea whether or not he would get the job, but if he didn't, well, the solution would be easy. If they asked him for another interview, and eventually gave him the job, he could always turn it down. If things continued to go well with Sean, he could stay here and be happy with him. If things went south with him, he would have a backup plan.

That was what he'd been missing before, and he felt better now that he had one. He knew Sean wouldn't be crazy about it, but also that he wouldn't argue. If this was what Peter wanted, he would support him, something that made Peter feel both guilty and happy.

Sean truly cared for him. Peter hadn't believed it in the beginning, mostly because even though they were mates, he couldn't understand how anyone could fall for someone so fast. Then he'd fallen for Sean, and now he knew exactly how it worked.

He heard the shower turn off, and he quickly put his phone down on the coffee table. He should talk to Sean about this, but he didn't want to ruin the evening. They were finally settling into a routine that felt like they'd been together for years rather than weeks, and Peter loved it.

He liked the solidity of it, of knowing what would happen. He didn't like surprises, so this was perfect for him.

He hoped it was perfect for Sean, too.

That was his main worry. Sean hadn't said anything about how they were behaving like an old married couple, sitting at home most evenings, eating dinner together, then watching TV. Peter loved it, but he understood it wasn't for everyone. Would Sean prefer to go out? Maybe see his family? Peter didn't know, but he suspected that if it was up to Sean, they'd already have had dinner with his brothers and his parents.

And Peter wanted to go. He was just nervous about it.

What if they didn't like him? Would that change the way Sean looked at him? And what if they liked him and he had to leave?

"Did something happen?" Sean asked, making Peter jump.

Peter's heart raced. He smiled at Sean, hoping his forced smile worked well enough. "I'm fine. Just a bit of a headache." It was the first excuse he could think of.

He regretted it when Sean grimaced and moved toward him. "Headache? When did it start? Why didn't you tell me before? I have some painkillers if you need them."

Sean was so considerate and loving. Peter loved him, but he couldn't tell him. Something was stopping him, and he knew what it was—he didn't fully trust that this could go on. He trusted Sean implicitly, even though he didn't understand why. He didn't trust the rest of the world, though. A lot of things could happen that would push them apart, and he was afraid.

"I'm fine. I just need some rest."

Sean didn't look reassured. "You should stay home tomorrow."

"You can't keep giving me vacation days. The others will get angry that you're giving me preferential treatment."

Sean smiled crookedly as he sat next to Peter. "They wouldn't be wrong. I *am* giving you special treatment. You're the one who sleeps with me in my bed, after all."

Peter's cheeks felt like they were on fire, and he looked away. "I'm not doing that because I work for you, though."

"True. But they like you, Peter. They wouldn't mind if you had to take a sick day."

"I don't think it'll be necessary, but thank you. You always think of everything."

Sean took one of Peter's hands and squeezed. "Only when it comes to you. I want to take care of you. I know you're not crazy about the idea, and I understand why. I just want you to know I'm here for you if you need anything. That includes painkillers, especially since we're supposed to have dinner with my family tonight."

Peter's eyes widened, and he pressed his lips together. He'd entirely forgotten about that. Sean had told him a few times, and Peter had agreed. He probably shouldn't have. Now, he would have to face them knowing that he might leave if he got the job that would take him away from Sean.

Sean's expression softened. "I can call them and reschedule if you don't feel okay. They'll understand."

"They're chomping at the bit to meet me. They've been waiting for weeks."

"That doesn't mean we have to go, though. If we don't, my mom will try to mother you from a distance, and I'll have to take some teasing because a few of my brothers think I'm imagining you, but I promise I'll be okay. If you're not feeling up to it, we're staying home."

It was tempting to say yes. It was tempting to stay in their comfortable bubble, but Peter knew he couldn't. If he and Sean were going to make this work, he would have to make compromises, and of course, he had to meet Sean's family. He supposed he was lucky the other way around wouldn't happen. Sean would never have to meet his parents, and he was happy about that. "I'll be fine. We can go," he said.

Sean stared at him for a moment. "If you're sure."

"I'm sure." Peter leaned closer to Sean and kissed him. He wasn't sure of much in his life, never had been. He *was* sure about how he felt about Sean, though.

Sean wasn't convinced that going to his parents' house was the best thing to do for Peter right then considering his headache, but Peter was an adult. He knew what he was agreeing to, so Sean wasn't going to push, especially since he'd already rescheduled a few times without telling Peter.

His mom had started inviting Peter over the day Peter had arrived in town. She wanted to meet him, even more so now that she knew he and Sean were mates and that they were together. Sean had kept her at arm's length until now, though. The last thing he wanted was for Peter to freak out, and that would have happened if they'd gone too soon. Sean knew his family. There were a lot of them, and they were all exuberant. A few were calmer, like Sean's twin, but the younger brothers would make a fuss, and Peter would feel self-conscious.

Sean was glad Peter wanted to meet his parents, though. He had everything he'd ever wanted — an apartment, and hopefully, one day, a home with Peter. He had a good job, and now, he had his mate. It didn't matter that Peter was still trying to find his bearings and get his feet under himself. They were working things out, and that was all that mattered. He could take some teasing if it meant he was with Peter.

Truthfully, he couldn't wait to introduce Peter to his family. They were a lot to deal with, especially in the beginning, but he wanted the two parts of his life to mesh together and to do it well. He was proud of Peter and their relationship.

He was also nervous, though. He and Peter belonged together, so he knew everything would be okay, but still. He couldn't help but wonder if this was how Curtis and Hugh had felt when they'd first introduced their mates to the clan. Had they wondered if everyone would like them? Well, everyone already liked Leon by the time they'd realized he was Hugh's mate, but when it came to Curtis, things had gone differently. He'd introduced Manuel to the family on Christmas day, but they'd quickly taken to him.

Manuel was good for Curtis. He was a quiet man, but he had strength, and he clearly adored Curtis. The relationship between Leon and Hugh had been a bit rockier in the beginning, but they'd worked through it, and now they were happy. Sean couldn't wait to have that kind of happiness with Peter. He knew they would eventually, but it was still early in their relationship. They had to work things out. He didn't mind.

"We can go whenever you're ready," Peter murmured.

He looked worried, and Sean suspected it was because he was about to meet his family. Anyone would have been worried about meeting their boyfriend's family, but things were more complicated when it came to mates. If they didn't get along, then Sean would have to make a decision and choose between his family and his mate. He didn't think he could make that kind of choice, and he knew that Peter understood that. He was probably terrified, since he was visibly jittery, but there was nothing Sean could tell him to make him feel better. They wouldn't know what would happen until they went, so they might as well go as soon as possible.

They headed out, and Sean kept an eye on Peter. Peter was bouncing his knee in the truck, staring out the window, his eyes wide. He looked startled, like a deer caught in headlights, and it made Sean wonder if his headache was possibly worse than he'd admitted to. They could still go home, or Sean could text to ask his mom to tell the others to be careful when they met Peter, which was what he did as soon as he parked in front of his parents' home. He hoped they would see the text before they swamped Peter, but if they didn't, he would play bodyguard to his mate.

"I love you," he said to reassure Peter.

Peter turned toward him. His eyes were even wider than before, and even though it was dark, Sean could see he was pale. "What if *they* don't? What will you do if they don't like me? I don't want you to have to choose between your family and me. It wouldn't be fair."

Those words echoed Sean's thoughts too closely for comfort. Sean didn't know what he would do if his family hated Peter, and he didn't want to live through that. There was one thing he was sure of, though—he would never leave his mate behind. "I don't care if they don't like you. The only important thing is whether or not *I* like you, and I do. You're in my life to stay. That is, if you *want* to stay."

Peter's expression shifted, but the emotions were moving too fast for Sean to read. "Of course I want that. I wouldn't be here if I didn't want to be with you."

"That's it, then. You're not going anywhere."

"I don't want to hurt you. I know what losing your family feels like, and it's horrible. I don't want that to happen to you."

Shit. Sean should have thought about it earlier. Of course Peter was afraid. The last time he'd faced a family, it had been his own, and his parents had kicked him out. They hadn't accepted him for who he was, and now, he was afraid that Sean's family would do the same.

Sean grabbed one of Peter's hands, holding it close, kissing his palm. He waited until he felt Peter relax. Then, he smiled at him. "I love my family," he began.

Peter shook his head. "I love my family, too, but *they* didn't love me enough."

"Let me finish?"

Peter stared at Sean for a moment before nodding curtly.

Sean nodded back. "Like I was saying, I love my family. I can't imagine my life without them in it. They've always been there. I've never been alone. Even after I was born, I had my twin brother. I don't want to lose them, but they also don't dictate my life and behavior, or who I love. I don't want to have to choose. It would be agonizing, and it would destroy me. But if I have to, I'll choose you."

"How can you say that? We barely know each other."

"I don't have to know you better to know that I love you and that I want to spend the rest of my life with you. I'm sure my family will accept that, and you, if not now, eventually. But my mom already loves you. You're not just Emily's brother, and she'd love you even only for that. You're also my mate. She wants you to feel welcome, and she'll do everything she can to make that happen."

"What if it's not enough? What if *I'm* not enough?" Peter's voice was soft, but Sean could hear the pain in it.

He should have realized the situation would bring Peter's mind back to his parents and what they'd done, and to the day they'd kicked him out. Now Peter had to meet Sean's entire family, and that was ten people if he didn't count himself. It was natural that Peter was freaking out. Hell, anyone would freak out at the thought of meeting all of those people at the same time, especially if they were related to their mate.

There was no way out of it, though. Well, they could still

back off and go home, but Sean had already noticed his mother staring at them from the kitchen window. She was doing her best not to be obvious, but she was almost bouncing on her feet, and he could tell how happy she was.

He could only hope it would continue. He truly thought Peter would get along with his family, especially after the initial awkwardness was over. He could only hope that Peter understood that, and that he'd do his best to get along with them. They would realize he was scared, and they would give him space. As long as he didn't push them away, things would be okay.

What if he pushed them away, though? It would be entirely understandable if he did, after what happened to his parents. Sean prayed it wouldn't happen, but he had to face the truth.

"We can still leave, if you feel more comfortable with that," he suggested.

Peter finally smiled. "I'm pretty sure your mom would sprint out of the house and grab us by the back of the neck." He sucked in a breath. "We should go in. They're waiting for us."

"Are you sure?"

"I'm sure. I want to meet your parents, Sean. They're part of your life, and I want to be, too."

He didn't realize that he already was, but that was okay. Sean had all the time in the world to make him see that.

Peter had to stop thinking about the interview and focus on Sean and his family. He was already nervous enough as it was. Thinking about the interview would only make things worse, and this was absolutely the worst moment for that to happen.

Peter had to relax and focus on what was happening now rather than what could happen next week or the week after that. He had to focus on making a good impression on Sean's family and making sure they liked him. No matter what Sean had told him, Peter didn't want him to have to choose. He didn't want him to lose his parents and his brothers. He had, and he was still hurting over it years later. He wanted Sean to be happy and to have his entire family with him, as well as Peter.

And he would do everything he could to make that happen.

He and Sean got out of the truck. Peter had noticed a woman standing behind one of the windows, and he knew it had to be Sean's mom. All the other members of Sean's family were males, even the mates, so there was no other explanation.

Peter knew he was right when the door flew open and she stood there, watching them. One of her hands was on her mouth, and her eyes were wide with tears. It made Peter slightly uncomfortable, but he plastered a smile on his face as they neared her.

Sean hooked an arm around Peter's waist and pulled him closer. "Ignore the tears. She's just happy for me. I know it's a lot, but my entire family is a lot."

"That's fine."

Sean chuckled. "It's really not. She's making a mountain out of nothing, and I know it makes you uncomfortable."

"I'm not going anywhere, no matter how I feel." It would take a lot more for Peter to run away from Sean's family.

"I know. And thank you for that."

By the time their short conversation was over, they were at the front door, and Sean's mom was still standing there, waiting. Peter suspected she wanted to hug him, but instead, she turned to Sean and wrapped her arms around him. "Welcome," she said when she was done, and she turned to Peter.

Peter offered her his hand, but he felt awkward. She was

almost vibrating with the need to hug him, so instead of shaking her hand, he opened his arms.

Sean's eyes widened and he mouthed *bad idea*, but before Peter could change his mind, Sean's mom threw herself at him. He had to wrap his arms around her to avoid both of them falling, and when he did, he relaxed.

It had been so long since he'd had gotten a mother's hug. It felt good, and it surprised him how much. He'd expected to feel uncomfortable, and he did, a little bit. It also felt good, though, and he knew he'd made the right decision coming here tonight.

"It's such a pleasure to meet you," Sean's mom said as she leaned back. "I've wanted to since I met your sister, but I didn't think it would happen this way."

"I doubt anyone thought it would happen this way. It's a pleasure to meet you, Mrs. Long."

She snorted. "Call me Mary. Mrs. Long was my mother-in-law, and even though I loved her, I feel much younger."

That made Peter smile. He wasn't surprised when Mary hooked an arm around his and pulled him inside. He *was* surprised at the wall of noise that hit him as soon as he stepped into the house.

He shouldn't have been. Sean had told him that his entire family would be here tonight, something that didn't often happen, usually only during the holidays. Apparently, though, they all wanted to meet Peter, and that included all of Sean's six brothers, his parents, and the two mates. It made Peter even more nervous to think about that, but he knew he could do this. The only other big hurdle he could see was meeting Sean's father, but if he was anything like Sean's mom, things would be okay.

They would have to be.

Mary pulled Peter into the living room, but he barely had time to look around the room before he was surrounded by men. They didn't touch him, but they stood around him, looking at him, offering him hands and talking to him. He didn't know where to start or look, and he was grateful when an arm hooked around his body and pulled him back. He hit Sean's chest, and Sean curled himself around him in a protective position as if he thought his brothers might mob Peter.

"Give him space, guys," Sean said with a growl that made something in Peter's stomach wiggle.

It had the effect Peter had been hoping for. Everyone took a step back, except for one man. He didn't look anything like Sean, so Peter suspected he was one of the mates. He was short and very colorful and gorgeous, with bright blue hair and blue nail polish. He was wearing makeup, and his nose ring glinted in the living room light. He was also beaming, as if he was truly happy to meet Peter.

Peter offered him his hand. "I'm Peter."

"Everyone knows who you are. I'm sure you don't know who I am, though. I'm Leon, Hugh's mate." He pointed his finger at a man Peter thought was Hugh. "He's Sean's twin, in case you're wondering."

Peter wasn't. Sean and Hugh were identical twins, so it was obvious. He shook Leon's hand, but before he could add anything, someone else was there, taking his place. "I'm Jack, Sean's brother. You'll be told that a lot tonight."

"You should probably put on nametags or something," Peter teased.

He realized it wouldn't have been a bad idea once man after man introduced themselves to him. He already knew their names from when Sean had talked about them, but there were a lot of them. He would have an easier time remembering Leon and Manuel, Curtis's mate, because they stood out. Laurie would also be easy since Peter had already met him, but the others looked so similar that they might have been twins, too. Peter knew their age went from Laurie's nineteen years old to Hugh and Sean's thirty-five, though, so he promised himself he would remember which brother was who.

Then, another stood in front of him. It had to be Richard, Sean's father. Peter knew he was human, but that he was aware that his wife and children were all swan shifters. He was smiling softly, and his grip was strong and warm when he shook Peter's hand. "It's a pleasure to meet you," he said. "I'm Richard."

"The pleasure is all mine."

Richard chuckled. "I'm pretty sure that's not the truth, but I'll act as if I believe you. I know it's a lot to meet all of us at the same time, and you weren't as lucky as the other two mates."

"I had to meet all of you for *Christmas*," Manuel pointed out, making everyone laugh.

Peter laughed, too. Yes, it was a lot, and he couldn't remember the names of half the people he'd just met, but this place felt like home. Sean was still hugging him, and everyone seemed happy to meet him.

He could imagine himself in this house for years to come, over for the holidays, chatting with everyone. He wanted it to happen. He *yearned* for it, and he knew what would happen after the interview. Even if they offered him the job, he would have to say no.

He would still go through with it, though. He wanted to prove to himself that he could do it and get the job. It might be awkward, and the people who would interview him wouldn't be happy about it if they found out, but he didn't care. He had to know if he could stand on his own two feet. Otherwise, he wouldn't be able to give himself to Sean. Once it was over, though, he would be Sean's for the rest of their lives.

Dinner had gone perfectly. Peter had relaxed, and now he was chatting with Manuel and Leon, his hands moving in front of him. Sean didn't think he'd seen him so carefree and happy unless they were alone, and he was glad that Peter felt at home here. He'd wanted it to happen, but he couldn't deny he'd freaked out a bit after their conversation in the truck.

He'd known his family would like Peter, and that even if they didn't, they wouldn't ask him to choose. They weren't like that. They knew how important mates were for shifters, and more importantly, they knew that Sean already loved Peter. They would have accepted him even if they hated him, but this made it so much easier.

Curtis grabbed Sean's shoulder. "You're not getting out of cleaning up just because you brought your mate," he pointed out.

Sean grinned at him. "It didn't work for you, so I don't see why I should think it would work for me."

"Just making sure. Come on. We'll be done quickly if we all help."

Laurie was the only one dragging his feet, but to Sean's surprise, he did help. He wasn't as upbeat as he usually was, and that made Sean worry. Laurie was only nineteen, still a teenager, and mostly, he acted like it. Maybe it was time for him to grow up a bit, though. With three brothers finding their mates, Laurie might find his, too. At this point, nothing would surprise Sean anymore. He thought that after two of his brothers meeting their mates, there would be no chances for the rest of them to do the same. Apparently, he'd been wrong, and Peter had come in his life. Who knew what fate reserved for his mateless four brothers?

"You and Peter look like you're doing okay," Richie said from his position at the sink where he was rinsing the dishes. He passed them to Jack, who put them in the dishwasher, while Andy, Laurie, and Hugh walked back and forth between the dining room and the kitchen, bringing in the dirty dishes. Sean and Curtis were on leftover duty, packing them into different containers so whoever wanted them could take them home.

"I'm happy. I never imagined this would happen, but I'm over the moon it did."

Richie groaned. "Am I going to be the next one? I'm not sure I want to meet my mate."

Laurie snorted. "I certainly don't."

It wasn't the first time they'd heard Laurie say that, but Sean still found himself asking, "Why not? Don't you want to meet someone you know you'll love forever?"

Laurie snorted. "I'm not crazy about having a mate. I don't want a mate who's been chosen for me by who knows who."

It made sense. Sean remembered that one of his brothers — maybe Curtis — had gone through that phase, too. No amount of telling Laurie he was wrong would change his mind, but that was okay. He was only nineteen.

"Well, you're probably the only one of us who's going to give Mom grandkids, so you should be careful," Andy teased him.

Laurie looked horrified. "I'm nineteen. I don't want children."

"You're also the only one of us who dates women. Actually, I don't think I've ever seen you with a guy. You're sure you're bisexual?"

Laurie crossed his arms over his chest and glared. "Who I date doesn't change my sexuality. I *am* bisexual, whatever you think."

Andy raised his hands in surrender. "Sorry. I didn't mean to doubt you."

Jack bumped his shoulder against Andy's. "He's more attracted to ladies than to guys. That's not a problem."

"I never said it was. I was just curious. I didn't mean

anything by it."

Sean sank into the familiarity of the conversation. His brothers always had something to bicker about. It made sense, since there was seven of them and their ages varied so much. Laurie was the baby brother, but some days, he felt almost like a son to Sean. Sean had been sixteen when Laurie had been born, so he *could* almost be his father. They'd been close when they were children, mostly because Sean had felt it was his duty to help his mom with all the kids since he was the oldest, but Laurie lived his own life now. Still, Sean inched closer to him, smiling at him when Laurie looked up. "You know no one cares, right?"

Laurie sighed. "I know. It's just that sometimes, I feel weird with you guys. I do like guys, but I mostly date women, and you're all on the other side of the spectrum."

"Again, no one cares who you sleep with. Sleeping with a woman comes with its own set of problems, though. We just want you to be happy and safe."

Laurie grimaced. "Dad already gave me the sex talk a while ago. You don't have to do it."

Sean hooked an arm around Laurie's neck and pulled him closer, kissing the top of his head before letting go. "I'm not about to do that. I just wanted you to know that we don't care who you're with and that we love you."

"Even though you're a little shit," Richie added.

They all laughed, and Sean relaxed. He didn't want his brothers to fight, and he was relieved they wouldn't. He truly didn't care who Laurie slept with, as long as he was careful. The last thing Laurie needed right now was a kid. He was only nineteen, and he had his entire life in front of him. Not that having a kid would ruin his life, but it *would* make things harder.

Peter was still talking with Manuel and Leon by the time the brothers were done cleaning the kitchen. He looked up when he heard them walk into the living room, and his smile told Sean everything he wanted to know.

He was relaxed. He looked happy and like he belonged. It was too easy for Sean to imagine both of them spending the holidays here, year after year, maybe even bring a few children into the mix in a few years. They would have to talk about it, but Sean felt more than ever that they could do this. He wanted them to be together forever, and he thought they had a pretty good chance of that happening.

"Ready?" he asked.

Peter shot up from the couch as if it had burned him. "Yes. We can go."

Leon laughed. "Eager to get back home, are you? I was that way, too, after I met Hugh."

"You're still that way," Manuel pointed out. They were best friends, but it was easy to see that Peter might become the third in their group.

Peter needed his own friends. Sean didn't have a lot of them, spending most of his time with his brothers or the people he worked with, but he wanted to give all of that to Peter. He wanted Peter to feel like he had a family again. It wouldn't be the same as having his parents, but hopefully, it would soothe him anyway.

It took them about twenty minutes to say their goodbyes to everyone. Sean ignored the smirks and winks, and he eventually had to drag Peter outside while he was still talking with Leon. The front door closed on laughter, and Sean took a deep breath. "That went well, didn't it?" he asked as they reached the truck.

"It did. Do you really want to go home? We can stay longer."

Sean looked at the sky, then at his mate. "Actually, I thought we could shift. I want to share my favorite spot with you."

"Oh. Of course. But you know, I usually shift in the apartment."

"I know." And he was adorable. Sean had caught him in the tub the other day, splashing around in a few fingers of water, and it had been too cute to be true.

Sean took one of Peter's hands and pulled him closer, kissing him. "So? Shifting?"

"Yes, please. I can't wait to do it outside. *That* has been a while. There's not really a place to do that in the city."

Sean should have thought about it sooner.

He drove them to his favorite spot. It was just a bunch of trees and some grass, but it was isolated. He always felt free when he was here. He knew he could go to his parents' home and shift in their backyard and that no one would see him, but there was always someone home, and his brothers were overwhelming on the best of days. Here, he had privacy and time to think. That was why he'd started coming here when he was a teenager. He'd wanted silence, and he'd gotten it. He didn't mind sharing with Peter, though. They were mates, and they would share everything.

"I love you," Sean told Peter as they got out of the truck.

Peter stumbled. "Did you really have to tell me now?" he asked.

Sean shrugged. "I just wanted you to know."

"You already told me before. Remember?"

Sean remembered, yes. He also remembered that neither that time nor now had Peter told him he loved him back.

It didn't matter. Peter hadn't run away when Sean had told him how he felt about him. Sean understood why Peter was careful with his feelings, and he didn't berate him for it.

He already knew Peter loved him. Now it was only a matter of time to wait for him to say the words out loud, and they had it.

"Ready to get naked?" he asked

He could tell Peter was blushing even though it was dark. He knew his mate well enough to be aware of his reactions, and he'd chosen his words for that purpose. Peter had relaxed over dinner, but now that it was over, Sean wanted his mate to focus on them.

"You make it sound like we're about to do something we shouldn't be doing in the open."

"Well, I don't know about you, but outdoor sex isn't my favorite thing. The last time it happened, I found a twig between my ass cheeks after I got home."

Peter dropped his t-shirt and glared at Sean. "Can we not talk about you having sex with someone who isn't me?"

Sean mimed locking his lips and throwing away the key. It made Peter laugh, but Sean focused on finishing taking off his clothes. He wanted to stare at his mate's naked body, but he didn't want to make his mate uncomfortable, and they didn't have long, because it was getting late.

He shifted right away and spread his wings, strutting a bit when he noticed Peter staring at him. Peter laughed again. Then, he shifted and scurried toward Sean, who opened his wing to allow him under there. He'd thought they could play around, but he didn't mind some cuddles before that happened.

Peter felt good against Sean's side, if a bit prickly. It reminded Sean of his personality and of the softness he hid under it. He stroked his feather down Peter's back, mentally grinning when Peter shivered. Then he bumped Peter's nose with his beak, making him squeak. Peter looked offended, and he stepped back only to turn around and run. Sean was pretty sure his mate wanted him to go after him, so he did.

He always would, as long as Peter wanted him to.

CHAPTER SIX

Peter didn't have a lot of time to do the interview. He was lucky he'd managed to schedule it during Sean's weekly grocery shopping run, But Sean would be back soon. Peter wanted to be done with the interview when he was, because that way he wouldn't have to give him an explanation. He didn't know what would happen, but he had to do this, and he didn't want to face Sean until he knew what the future held.

He smiled at his computer screen. "Good afternoon," he said.

The woman on the other side smiled back at him. "Good afternoon. Let's begin, shall we?"

Peter nodded tightly. He was ready for this, or at least, as ready as he ever would be.

The interview didn't last long, just over fifteen minutes. It had been a while since he'd gone through one, but he thought he'd done well, and he didn't know how that made him feel. He was relieved when he was able to close his computer, and even more so when he took off his suit jacket and dress shirt — and the tie. That was the one thing he didn't miss about working in an office. At least he'd been able to keep his legs clad in sweats, which were infinitely more comfortable than dress pants.

He'd just changed when he heard the front door open. He swallowed, eyeing his computer. He'd managed to do everything he had to do without Sean noticing, but now, he was going to have to be careful. Sean couldn't find out about this, not yet, possibly not ever.

Peter doubted he would get the job. It was for a big firm, something he would have jumped on if he'd still been in Boston on his own. Hell, he was kind of tempted to go if he got the job. He might have if he hadn't met his mate. There was no way he was leaving Sean behind, though. He'd done the interview to prove himself that he could do it, that he could be independent even after everything that happened.

The guest bedroom door slammed open, but instead of Sean, it was Emily. She grinned and threw herself into Peter's arms.

Peter hugged her back, even though he was stunned. "What are you doing here?" he asked before kissing the top of her head.

"What do you *think* I'm doing here? I'm here to see you, stupid." Emily leaned back and kissed his cheek. Then, she looked at the bed, and she noticed Peter's shirt and suit jacket.

She narrowed her eyes, and Peter knew he would have to give her an explanation. He was tempted to tell her he was just cleaning up or something like that, but he doubted she would believe him. She knew him too well.

"What's going on?" she asked, taking a step back. "I thought you were staying in Sean's bedroom."

Peter sighed. He'd almost done it. He'd almost managed to get away with it, and now he would have to explain.

He sighed. "I am. Some of my stuff is still here, though." Mostly the stuff he wasn't using like his suits. "If I tell you, you have to promise me not to tell Sean."

Emily scrunched her nose. "He's my best friend. I don't want to hide things from him."

"And I'm your brother. I won't tell you anything if you can't make that promise. It's nothing bad, at least not the way you seem to think." Peter wanted to tell Sean himself — if there was anything to tell him when all of this was over.

"You do realize that you saying that makes me wonder, though, right?"

"I'll explain. I promise. But you can't tell Sean. I want to be the one to do it."

She sighed and sat on the bed. "Fine. I promise. Now tell me."

Peter bit his lower lip. He paced the room, wondering how to say it. Then, he decided he might as well just say the words and see what happened. "I had a job interview. That's why I wore the jacket and shirt, and the tie."

Emily beamed. "Really? That's great! Is it in town? Makes me wonder why you couldn't do it face to face."

"It *is* good."

"How did it go?" She paused and frowned. "Where's the job, Peter?"

This was where things would get dicey. "In Boston."

Emily frowned. "What do you mean?"

"You heard me. The job I interviewed for is in Boston."

Emily rose from the bed. "Does that mean you're going to leave Sean behind? Are you breaking up with him?"

"I don't know what I'm doing. I just wanted to do the interview. I don't even know if I got the job. I doubt it."

"And if you did? What's going to happen then?"

"I don't want to think about it right now. Please, Emily. There's no need to freak out. I never said I was going to leave. I don't think I would, even if I get the job. But I had to prove to myself that I could do it."

Emily's expression softened. She got to her feet, then, to Peter's surprise, she hugged him again. "I can't say that I know how you feel, but it can't be easy for you to have your life change that much so quickly. So yes, I understand." She stepped back and grimaced. "I still think you should talk to Sean about it. He won't be happy if he finds out when you're ready to leave."

"I don't know if I'm going to leave. I don't want to."

"Yet you went through with the interview."

"Only to prove I could do it. I don't think I'll go anywhere. If I find another job, it's going to be here, in town. I already have a few interviews lined up." It wouldn't be the same, but Peter didn't think it was a bad thing. He'd come to enjoy the slower rhythm of a small town.

"Okay. I think I understand."

"Do you?" It would be a relief if she did.

"You're worried. I get it. And it's fine. You wanted to prove something, and now, you did. Right?"

"I haven't proven anything yet, but yeah. That was all I was planning on doing. I don't want to hurt Sean. He's too important to me."

"I won't tell him anything. I promise."

"I'll tell him." Eventually. Even though Peter wasn't planning on going anywhere, it wouldn't be easy to confess this to Sean. He didn't even know why except for the fact that he knew his mate would be disappointed, both that Peter had considered leaving and that he hadn't confided in him.

"Even if you don't get the job?"

Emily truly knew Peter too well. "Even then. I swear I'm not planning on leaving. I just found him. Why would I want to go?"

Emily finally smiled. It was more natural, and it made Peter feel better. "All right. I'll trust you on that. And I'll make sure not to mention any of this to Sean."

"Thank you."

"Are you sure you won't take the job if you get it?"

She was still worried, then. "I doubt I'll get it, but I promise I'm not going anywhere. I can't lose Sean, not now that I just found him, and hopefully, not ever. I don't *want* to lose him and be alone again."

Emily nodded, and Peter hoped that was it. He didn't want

to explain himself even further.

"What about *you*? What are you doing here?" he asked Emily, hoping to distract her.

"I told you. I wanted to see you. It was about time, too."

"Does Sean know you're here?" Peter hadn't heard him come in, which could be a problem.

"It's a surprise. I didn't expect to be able to get away from my job this soon, but I have a key, and it won't be the first time he comes home to find me here."

Peter beamed. "And what a surprise. I'm happy to see you."

Emily hooked an arm around Peter's waist. "I'm glad I came, too. I'm pretty sure you would be in trouble if I hadn't."

Just then, the front door opened again, and Peter knew she was right. She winked at him, then gestured at the shirt on the bed. "Put that way. I'll distract him."

"Thank you."

"There's nothing to thank me for. You're my brother. Sean might be my best friend, but I'll always be on your side — as long as you're not intentionally cruel."

Peter was relieved to hear that.

Emily was the first thing Sean saw as he walked into the apartment. He almost dropped his grocery bags, but he managed to get them to the kitchen counter before turning around and opening his arms.

Emily threw herself into them. He wrapped them around her, surprised and happy to see her. "What are you doing here?" he asked, burying his face in her hair. She smelled like strawberries, just like always, and it was familiar and soothing.

Emily poked Sean in the ribs. "What do you think I'm doing here? I wanted to see my two favorite people in the world." She leaned back and beamed. "I still can't believe the two of you are together. I wish I'd introduced you a long time ago."

Sean smiled and kissed her forehead. "We might not have been in the right place to be together if you had. I think things went the way they were supposed to go."

Emily wrinkled her nose. "If you say so. You're not going to make me change my mind, though. You and Peter could have been happy a long time ago, and I feel it's my fault you weren't."

"You didn't do anything wrong." Sean knew that both Peter and Emily had the tendency of thinking everything was their fault. He didn't want them to, especially not when it came to his relationship with Peter.

Peter had followed his sister into the kitchen and was looking at them with a smile playing on his lips. He turned his attention to Sean, and his smile widened. "It was a surprise for me, too. I was putting away some clothes in my room, and the door flew open and she walked in. I almost had a heart attack."

Sean stepped away from Emily and hooked an arm around Peter's waist, pulling him closer. "I'm glad you didn't. I don't want you to lose you so soon."

Peter leaned closer. "I don't want to lose you at all."

When Sean looked at Emily, she was staring at them with hearts in her eyes and a sappy expression. Sean rolled his eyes at her. "So, do you want to go out for dinner since you're here?" he asked.

"Or we could cook," Peter suggested.

Emily's terrified expression told Sean she didn't want to taste his cooking. She'd been his guinea pig too many times, and it had never ended well. "I think dinner out will be good for all three of us. We can catch up without having to think about washing dishes."

"Fine. I'll go wash up. You two be good," Peter said. He patted Sean's chest, then headed to the bedroom.

Their bedroom.

Even though technically Peter was still staying in the guest room, as soon as they'd started sleeping together, he'd moved into the master bedroom. They hadn't spent one night apart since that day, and Sean hoped that would continue. He didn't like that Peter had said it was his room, but he understood Peter used it to keep most of his clothes and the few things he'd managed to save from the flooding of his apartment. Sean wished Peter would transfer everything to his bedroom and the rest of the apartment, but he hadn't yet asked. Peter would do it when he was comfortable, and that was that.

Emily leaned against the counter, watching as Sean finally moved to put away the groceries. "So, what do you think about the jobs Peter is considering?"

Sean almost dropped the eggs. He didn't, thankfully, and he put them away before he turned to Emily. "What jobs?"

Emily bit her lower lip. "He hasn't talked to you about it?"

"I know he's been looking for jobs, but I didn't know he was considering any of them."

Emily peered at the door. "Okay, so he told me not to tell you, but—"

"Then you shouldn't. If you promised, you need to keep that promise."

"And I want to. I would if I didn't think he was messing things up. He had an interview for a job in Boston."

Sean hadn't wanted Emily to tell him, and he hadn't changed his mind now that he knew. Why was Peter considering jobs in Boston? Did he want to leave? What would that mean for them?

And more importantly, why hadn't Peter told him he was looking for a job so far away from him?

Sean couldn't answer that question, but he suspected Peter hadn't told him because he hadn't wanted to. He'd probably been afraid of Sean's reaction, and Sean didn't like that. He knew Peter wasn't afraid of him, but still. He wanted them to be able to talk about everything and anything and he wasn't happy about Peter keeping secrets, not *this* kind of secret.

He shook his head. "You shouldn't have told me. He made you promise, and you broke that promise."

Emily's expression turned stubborn, and she crossed her arms over her chest. "It's not the first time I broke one of the promises I made to my brother, and it won't be the last. Look, Sean, I wouldn't have said anything if I thought he was doing the right thing, but I don't."

"What happened to make you think that?"

"He'd just finished that interview when I came in. I used my key, so he didn't know I was there. He promised he would tell you whether or not he got the job, but I know him. He thinks he has to make all the decisions on his own, and he doesn't want to include you in it. It's going to create problems between the two of you, and I don't want that to happen."

"You don't know what's going to happen. He told you he'd talk to me." But Sean couldn't help but wonder if Peter would have.

Emily wasn't wrong. Peter was a private man, which made sense, since he didn't trust people. His parents, the two people he should have been able to trust, had kicked him out. How was he supposed to trust anyone else not to do that? How was he supposed to trust anyone enough to open up to them?

Sean didn't have an answer to that, but he wished Peter would see that he would never betray his trust. Of course, he probably thought the same of Emily, yet here she was, spilling the beans even though she'd promised not to.

Sean shook his head. "You shouldn't have told me," he

repeated. "I'm sure there's a good reason for Peter not to tell me."

"Well, he said he just wanted to show to himself that he could do it," Emily added.

That made sense, too. Peter had lost a lot in a short amount of time. He wanted to stand on his own two feet, and he was ready to do anything he could to make that happen.

Maybe even move away.

Sean didn't want to come to conclusions without talking to Peter, but it was hard not to. Why would Peter have gone through with the interview if he weren't considering accepting the job? Sean wanted to believe Emily when she said that Peter just wanted to prove to himself that he could do it, but there was an inkling of doubt in the back of his mind.

He and Peter had rushed into their relationship. Sean was aware of it, and he didn't care. He loved Peter, and he wanted to spend the rest of his life with him. He realized that they didn't know each other that well yet, though, and he didn't know what to make of Emily's words. She was Peter's sister, probably the person who knew him best in the world. If she thought he wouldn't have talked to Sean, then maybe she wasn't wrong.

Or maybe she was. Maybe she'd broken Peter's trust for nothing. Sean had no way to know unless he asked Peter, and he didn't want to do it now. He didn't want to ruin the evening, not when Emily wouldn't be staying long. She never did.

He rubbed his face. "Right now, I hate you a bit," he told her.

She stepped closer and hugged him again. "I know. I hate myself a little bit, too. I still think I was right to do it, though. I don't know if Peter really believes himself when he says he was only trying to prove to himself that he could do it, but I don't, not entirely. Maybe he thinks that's the case, but will he really turn down the job if he gets it?"

Sean didn't have an answer to that except for the uncomfortable churning in his stomach.

Something was wrong. Peter didn't know what it was, but he wanted to find out.

He'd realized something was going on as soon as he'd left the bedroom and found Sean and Emily still in the kitchen. They'd been talking, but they'd stopped when they'd noticed him.

That probably meant they'd been talking about him.

He didn't know about what, though. He couldn't help but wonder if Emily had broken his trust. He didn't want to think that of his sister, but it was a possibility. He loved Emily, but she had never been great at keeping secrets, especially when she thought it was wrong to keep it. She might have talked to Sean, although Peter didn't want to consider that possibility.

And now, here they were, sitting around a table, all three of them silent as they ate their food. Peter wanted things to change, but could they? Was there anything he could say to make Sean smile? To make Emily look less worried?

He forced himself to smile. "Has Sean told you about that time I tried to help put up a wall?" he asked Emily.

Emily's smile was as fake as Peter's felt. "He hasn't. Tell me about it."

Peter turned to Sean to involve him in the conversation, but Sean was focused on his plate, and he didn't even look up at Peter.

Peter tried to make the story funny because it had been when it had happened. It wasn't working, though.

Sean was quiet, and Emily looked like she'd done something wrong. Peter wanted to think she hadn't, but the proof was right in front of him. He couldn't yell at her, not when they were in public and he wasn't a hundred percent sure, but he knew she would probably confess as soon as they left the restaurant, and he couldn't wait.

He hoped his sister had kept his secret. He'd needed her to, but it looked like she'd gone straight to Sean and told him everything. Peter was angry, both at Emily and at himself. Mostly at himself, though.

He shouldn't have gone through with the interview. He shouldn't even have applied for the job, although he'd done it before he and Sean had gotten together. Now, everything was ruined, and he didn't know what to do.

Peter was relieved when they left the restaurant, at least until Sean asked Emily, "Did you take your stuff up to the apartment?"

She blinked at him as if she didn't understand what he was saying. "I left everything in my car."

"Why? You can have the guest room. Peter's been staying with me lately."

Emily shook her head. "I'm going to a bed and breakfast."

Peter didn't like the thought of her not doing what she usually did. He wouldn't have had a problem with her staying in the guest room in any other situation, and he wanted her to, but he also wanted to talk things out with Sean, and he doubted he could do it with his sister right next door.

"You always stay in the guest room when you come here," Sean said.

"I know, but you've never had a boyfriend when I did."

"Peter's not my boyfriend."

"No. He's your mate, which is one more reason for me to stay away. Besides, I think you need to talk."

Sean nodded curtly but didn't look at Peter. "We do."

Peter was *sure* something had happened now. He didn't want Emily to leave them alone. He was afraid of what would happen if she did. He also knew that Emily and Sean were right, though. He and Sean needed to talk, and he had to explain. Hopefully, Sean would understand. Peter didn't know what would happen if he didn't.

The three of them stayed silent as they drove back to Sean's apartment. Emily was looking out the window, while Peter was jittery. He kept bouncing his knee, then catching himself and trying to stop. It only took a few seconds for him to start again, though, and he felt like he was about to jump out of his skin by the time they got to their building. Sean parked, then he turned to look at Emily. "Do you want me to drive you to the bed and breakfast?"

"I can get there my own. I have my car, don't I?"

"Yes, but you're not familiar with the town."

"I'm familiar enough to know where the bed and breakfast is. Don't worry about me, Sean. I'll be fine." She turned her attention to Peter, and her guilty expression told Peter he'd been right. "Everything will be okay," she murmured.

Peter wasn't sure that was the case, but what could he say?

He slid out of the truck after his sister, then turned to face her. "I know what you did," he murmured while Sean was on the other side of the vehicle.

Emily looked away. "I'm sorry, yet I'm not."

"You promised," Peter hissed.

"I know, and I feel horrible for breaking that promise. I don't feel sorry about it, though. It was the right thing to do."

"How can you say that? You saw how dinner went. Was that really how you thought the evening would go when you came here?"

"No, but then I didn't think you were looking for jobs away from Sean. I love you, Peter. You're my brother, and I'm usually on your side — but not this time. This time, *you're* wrong."

"You're on Sean's side."

"I'm on the *right* side. You're going to hurt him if you don't talk to him, and I know you. You wouldn't have said anything unless you had to."

"I promised you I would."

"And people always keep their promises, don't they?"

Peter snorted, but he knew Emily was aware of what she'd said, and she didn't back down.

"You can hate me all you want, but if this will help you and Sean stay together, I don't care. I'll do it again if I have to. I love both of you, Peter. I can't choose."

"So you went and betrayed me."

"I did. If you think about it, though, you'll see that I was right. You were never going to tell him about the job, not if you didn't get it."

"You can't know that."

"I do know *you*, though. I know my brother. I know you're hurting, and that you don't feel you can trust anyone, but you're wrong. You *can* trust Sean. Tell him about the job. Tell him why you decided to go through with the interview, and what you expect to happen. He'll understand."

Peter stepped closer to her. Sean was still in the truck, apparently looking at his phone, but he was giving Peter and Emily time to talk things out. Peter was both grateful and annoyed. He wanted Sean to come out with it, to yell at him for what he'd done, to make it obvious that he was angry. Instead, Peter had to deal with his sister, and it wasn't something he wanted to do right now.

"It's obvious I distrust people. They break my trust when I give it to them."

Emily flinched, but she looked just as convinced as she had before. "You can hate me all you want. I still think I did the right thing, and I don't regret it, not if it keeps you and Sean together." She took a step toward her car. "I should go. I have to give the two of you time to talk things out. And you *will* do it, Peter. You have to. I don't know if Sean is going to force this conversation, but if he doesn't, you have to bring it up. He already knows. Don't let this become a hurdle in your relationship. It's not worth it."

She was right, even though Peter didn't want to admit it. Right now, he didn't want to admit anything to Emily.

She'd broken his trust, just like his parents had. It wasn't the same thing because their break of trust had been much worse than Emily's, but Peter wasn't sure he could forgive her.

Now wasn't the time to think about that, though. He had to focus on Sean and making things right with him, and he didn't know if he would be able to.

He didn't know if, by the end of the evening, he'd still have Sean in his life – or Emily.

Sean didn't know how to bring up the conversation he'd had with Emily to Peter. He knew he had to, though. Things hadn't been right between them since he and Emily had that conversation in the kitchen, and Sean didn't like it.

He liked the thought of Peter leaving even less.

He didn't want Peter to go. He wanted his mate to stay with him, but if this was what Peter wanted, then Sean wouldn't try to stop him – much.

He wanted Peter to be happy. If Peter couldn't be while living here with Sean, then Sean would have to let him go.

They both watched Emily drive away. Then they headed toward the building, still silent. He should probably just say the words and see what happened. He could tell Peter was angry at Emily. He understood why, too. Emily had promised Peter she wouldn't say anything, and then, as soon as he'd turned around, she'd blurted out the entire story to Sean. Peter felt betrayed, and he was right to. Emily *had* betrayed his trust. Sean hoped that didn't mean the siblings would stop talking. He didn't want to be the cause of them fighting and losing each other. He didn't want to lose either of them or to have to choose a side.

He loathed not knowing what would happen. He was a planner, and Peter's entrance into his life had thrown everything into disarray. He didn't mind, or rather, he *hadn't* minded. Now, he found that he wanted to find out what was going on and what would be next. It was the only way for him to plan, and hopefully, to shield his heart.

They got to their front door. Peter looked like he was about to explode, so maybe Sean wouldn't have to say anything. He was right because as soon as they stepped into the apartment and the door closed behind them, Peter turned to him. "Why aren't you saying anything?" he asked.

"What do you expect me to say?"

"I don't know. Tell me what's wrong. Do you want me to go? I will if it makes you feel better."

Sean shook his head. He should have known that Peter would think he wanted Peter to leave. He didn't, though. It was the last thing he wanted. "Emily told me about your job interview."

Peter nodded curtly, his expression tight. "She shouldn't have. She promised me she wouldn't, then she turned around and betrayed me."

"Did she tell you why she did it?"

Peter sighed, and his shoulders slumped. He looked more tired than angry now, and Sean hoped it was a good thing. "She said she didn't think I would tell you, especially if I didn't get the job."

"And would you have?"

"I don't know. I promised her I would, but it would have been easier to ignore everything, especially if I didn't get the job."

"Did you? Get the job, I mean."

Peter shrugged. "I had the interview today, so it could be a while before I find out."

"Do you want to tell me why you did it?" And why he hadn't told Sean, but Sean didn't ask that question.

Peter nibbled on his lower lip, something he did to gather his thoughts. Sean gave him the time he needed. It couldn't be an easy situation for Peter, and it wasn't for Sean, either. They could both say things that would hurt the other and regret it, but once those words were out there, it would be too late. It was better not to say them to begin with, but that meant they couldn't yell at each other and fight. They had to be adults about it, talk things out, and Peter had to be the one who started.

He sighed heavily and flopped onto the couch. "I didn't mean for any of this to happen," he started.

"Nothing has happened yet, Peter." Sean settled onto the coffee table so he could look at Peter. It creaked a bit, making both of them smile, but the smiles were quickly gone.

Peter nodded. "I know. Something *will* happen, though. I don't know what yet, and I would hate myself if I ruined everything you and I have."

"I can't promise you it won't happen because I don't know what's going on, but I *can* tell you that I love you and that it's going to take a lot to push me away. You're my mate, Peter, but more importantly, you're the man I love. Unless you betrayed me badly, I'm not going anywhere."

Peter stared at Sean. "I wish I could believe that," he murmured.

Sean wanted to reach for him, but he didn't know if it was a good idea, or if Peter would allow it. "I want you to trust me. I realize we haven't known each other long enough for you to, but I'm truly not going anywhere. I'm not your parents, Peter. I'm not going to kick you out because you tell me something I don't like. Try me. Please."

Peter rubbed his face with both his hands. "I was surprised when I applied for that job and I didn't expect it to hear back.

It's one of the big firms, and I applied there more than once in the past couple of years. They never even answered. I didn't think they would this time, either, but they did. I had to do the interview."

"Why?" Sean asked, even though Emily had already told him. He wanted Peter to be the one to explain.

"Because I lost so much. I feel like everything I worked for my entire life is gone. I lost my job and my apartment. I had to move away. I lost my family. I don't have anything left, or rather, I didn't have anything until I found you. But even though you gave me everything I needed, I feel like I might lose it if I lose you. I don't want to depend on you. I never want to depend on anyone."

"You don't. You have a job. You're paying bills."

"But we both know that I wouldn't have a job if it weren't for you. I love you for helping me, especially since you didn't even know me when you agreed to it, but I can't allow you to continue doing it."

"I already knew that, Peter. I also know you've been applying for jobs around town." Sean had thought *all* of them were in town, but clearly, he'd be wrong.

"And I haven't heard back from any of them yet. Besides, I didn't apply for this job for the same reason."

"You applied for that one because you wanted to prove to yourself that you could do it," Sean said slowly.

"Exactly. I had to prove to myself that if I wanted to, I could go, and I would still have a job and a home. I wanted to prove to myself that if I left you, too, I wouldn't die, that I wouldn't just curl into a tight ball and fade away. I wanted to prove to myself that I could stand up on my own, that I could survive no matter who I lost."

The words hit Sean hard. Emily had explained all of this, and he knew where Peter was coming from, but it was different to hear it from his mate's lips. "What will you do if you do get the job?" Sean asked. That was the question, wasn't it? No matter the reason Peter had applied to the job, the only thing that mattered was what he would do if he got it.

Peter shook his head, and Sean's stomach dropped. He expected Peter to tell him he would have to go. It would make sense. If this truly was a dream job for Peter, he had to take it.

"I wasn't sure what I was going to do for a long time," Peter admitted. "I don't think I'll get the job. I truly don't. I didn't the other times, and this isn't any different."

"But you might get it. You have more experience now."

"I do. But it's not my dream job anymore."

Sean didn't want to hope, not yet. "Why not?"

"I'm not sure. Maybe because I only had my job before. But I have you now. I have your family and the people we work with. I don't know if I trust them yet, but I know I'm not alone anymore. I only had my job to focus on in the past, but doing that now would take a lot away, including you. And I don't want to lose you, Sean." He leaned forward, taking one of Sean's hands in his and squeezing. "I want what we have to work. I know you do, too. I was stupid not to tell you about the interview, but I was afraid that you'd jump to the wrong conclusions." He smiled deprecatingly. "And you might not have been wrong. I thought about it, though, and I know what I'm going to do. *If* they offer me the job, I'll decline the offer. I filled out more than enough applications in town to find something, and if I don't, well, I can work for you until I do. You won't get rid of me easily, Sean."

Sean finally allowed himself to smile. "Good. Because I don't want to get rid of you. If I have my way, you won't leave my side for the rest of our lives."

When Peter smiled, Sean knew that he had been telling the truth. No matter what he'd done and why, he wasn't going anywhere.

CHAPTER SEVEN

Peter was putting away the last of his clothes into Sean's dresser — or rather, *their* dresser — when his phone pinged with an email. He snatched it from the top of the dresser, looking at it but not expecting much. It was probably his sister, apologizing once again, or maybe one of Sean's brothers. Peter didn't know where they'd gotten his number, but they'd started texting him, and they'd included him in the family chat.

That had been a weird experience. Peter had never had a family chat, and it was overwhelming. He'd had to mute the notifications because it kept pinging, and it was driving him crazy. It was oddly soothing and reassuring to know that he was able to open the chat and read the messages anytime he wanted, though. So far, he'd only participated a few times, but no one had pushed him, and he knew they wouldn't. They were giving him all the time he needed to get used to it, and he was grateful.

It wasn't the family chat, though. It was an email from the job he'd applied for in Boston, the one for which he'd done the interview. He stared at it, wondering what he should do.

He and Sean had talked about it more than once. After that first night when they'd been overly emotional, they'd wanted to talk things out, and they had. Sean had explained why he'd freaked out, and Peter had once again told him why he had done it. He realized that he should have talked to Sean before he did, but he still didn't feel guilty about the fact that he hadn't. He'd needed time, and he knew that Sean would have

110

given it to him if he'd asked for it.

They were compromising, finding their way around each other, and they both knew it would take time. They were meshing two lives together, and for Peter especially, it was hard. Ever since his parents had disowned him, he'd been on his own. He had Emily, but she lived in another city, so it wasn't the same. Peter hadn't needed to include her in his life beyond a few phone calls and texts. Sean was always there, though. He was there every evening and every morning, every time Peter thought about the future. Peter *had* to include him, and he was more than happy to. It would take some time to get used to it, though, and he was still working on it.

He opened the email. Staring at it wouldn't help, and he needed to know what was going on. He'd promised Sean that he wouldn't take the job, and he still wasn't planning on doing it, even though he doubted he'd gotten it.

He had.

He quickly read the email. They were offering him the job, with a substantial yearly salary. If he accepted, he would out-earn every job he'd ever had. That included the one he still had with Sean, and he knew Sean wouldn't be happy about it. Knowing him, he would probably try to give Peter a raise, but Peter wouldn't allow that to happen.

So he'd gotten the job. He was happy, satisfied, but not over the moon like he would have been a few months ago. Even though he knew he could do it now, he was going to decline.

"Everything okay?" Sean asked as he walked into the bedroom. He was holding a laundry basket with folded clothes in it, and he put in on the bed once he saw Peter's expression.

Peter handed him the phone so he could see what was going on. Sean took it and read it, his frown deepening as he read through the email. Then, he looked up at Peter. "I knew you could do it," he murmured.

"I got the job."

"What now?"

Sean was hesitant, even though he shouldn't be. They'd gone through this. They'd talked about it. Besides, Peter had a surprise for him, and it had nothing to do with this job offer. "No, I'm going to email them back and tell them that I'm grateful for the offer, but I can't take it," Peter said.

Sean hesitated. He handed Peter's phone back, then asked, "Are you sure?"

"I am. We already talked about this, remember?"

"I do, and I know you said you were going to turn it down. I don't want you to resent me, though. I know you don't like working for me, and what they're offering you is an incredible opportunity. I'm proud of you."

"I won't resent you. I *would* resent myself for taking it if I have to leave you behind, though. I won't let that happen. I'm staying, Sean. I told you it would take a lot to get rid of me, and it's still true." He stepped closer, wrapping his arms around Sean's neck. "Besides, I already found another job."

Sean blinked. "You have?"

"I did, and I accepted it. I'm not going anywhere, Sean. I promise."

Peter knew this was the right thing to do, both for himself and his relationship with Sean. He'd had doubts until now, but he didn't anymore. Sean's willingness to let him go if that was what he wanted had sealed the deal. He couldn't abandon his mate.

He wouldn't regret it. He could do everything he wanted now, and he was going to. In this case, what he wanted wasn't to take this great job he'd applied for but rather take another, smaller, not as well paid, one in a small town. Being here meant that he would be able to stay with Sean, and that was all that mattered.

Peter had focused on his job for too many years. It had

made the pain easier to deal with, and his parents' betrayal smoother to swallow down. It had been easier because Peter hadn't had to think about them. He hadn't had to confront his own feelings about everything, but now, he had, and he knew that no matter what they'd done, he hadn't deserved it.

He did deserve Sean, though, and everything that came with him. He deserved to be loved. More importantly, *Sean* deserved to be trusted. He hadn't done anything that had broken Peter's trust. He'd be there for Peter every time Peter had needed him, and that would never change. His family was there, too, supporting and loving. They'd welcomed Peter in their ranks, never pushing for anything. They wanted him to feel like he belonged, and he finally did.

He'd never felt that way with his parents. He'd been hurt by their rejection, and when he thought about it, he still was. He still didn't understand how they'd been able to push him away, and he knew he never would. He couldn't change the way his parents thought or what they told him, and he wasn't planning on trying. He was done trying. He didn't believe anything they'd told him, or that he didn't deserve any of this.

He deserved it. He deserved all of it—Sean's love, the family they were building, the friends he'd found when he'd started working for his mate. The home they would have together as soon as they started looking for it.

Peter had wanted to know if he could stand on his own two feet, and he could. He didn't have to, though, and that was the most important thing he'd realized. He'd taken a leap of faith, and Sean had caught him.

Sean loved him. He loved Sean. The fact that they were together meant that they could rely on each other in a way Peter never had done and had never understood. He did now, though, and he was going to take advantage of it.

He could rely on Sean, and Sean could rely on him. That was what being a couple meant, and he couldn't wait to see what was next for them.

You may also enjoy the following from eXtasy Books Inc:

Julian
Catherine Lievens

Excerpt

Julian looked around, his hands on his hips. The warehouse was a mess after the attack, and it hurt to see it. He hadn't been staying here long, but everyone had made him feel welcome, and he would miss the place. He didn't know what was next for him—he was with the assassins for protection, but now he wanted to stay with them.

No one would be staying in the warehouse, though. They couldn't, not when someone had found it. It had been attacked, and it wasn't safe anymore. That meant they had to find a new place to stay, and since Julian wasn't part of the assassins or a mate, he didn't know what would happen to him.

Well, he was a mate, but not of one of the assassins. He was Tali's mate, and Tali was one of the Nix who worked in the infirmary. Julian didn't know if that would be enough for the assassins to allow him to stay indefinitely, but he hoped so, even though he knew they'd always choose Tali over him.

He wanted to help the assassins find out who did this and

take them out. He wanted to have a chance with Tali, even though he didn't understand why his mate was keeping him at arm's length. More importantly, he didn't want to be alone anymore. He also had to be safe, which wouldn't happen until he found out who was after him and why.

He supposed he could survive on his own. He had for a long time, and he was more than capable. The fact that he didn't want to be on his own anymore was important, though. He could get in trouble, and someone would come to help him.

Maybe.

He still wasn't sure what most of the assassins thought of him, but he supposed he was lucky they weren't kicking him out.

"What are you doing, standing there?" Roark asked him as he passed by him.

"I'm not sure. I guess I was looking at the damage."

Roark rolled his eyes and straightened an armchair. "There's no reason for you to look at the damage. Go to your bedroom and grab whatever you need. It's why we're here for."

It was, but it looked like Roark had trouble doing what he'd just told Julian to do. He was moving furniture, picking up things, and looking around as if his heart had been torn out of his chest.

He'd lived here a lot longer than Julian. He'd been an assassin, and now, he was in charge of them. This was his home. Seeing it destroyed, knowing that people had invaded it, had to hurt.

Julian wanted to help, but he didn't know how. He and Roark weren't friends—far from it. Julian had been angry at Roark for killing one of the people he'd been hired to kill, which meant he hadn't been paid for it and he'd had to listen to his handler yelling at him. Julian had wanted to kill Roark for the slight, but he hadn't been able to. He'd tried a few times, but instead of killing him, he'd found himself fascinated by the way Roark and the others interacted. He'd never thought that an assassin could have friends, not the way Roark did. The assassins worked together, of course, but they were also family, and it had made Julian's heart ache.

It still did.

He wasn't part of the assassins or their family. Now that the warehouse was gone, he would have to find a motel or go to his family. He didn't want to pull them into it, but it would be better than being on his own. Of course, the people after him might be able to find him there, which meant they would be in danger, too. They were more than able to deal with it, but Julian didn't want them to have to. He didn't want them to know he'd failed.

"How are you doing?" Roark asked gruffly.

Julian blinked at him. "I'm fine." Julian hadn't been hurt, but he was confused. Over only a few hours, the warehouse had been attacked, he'd fought against the attackers, he'd been shimmered to Gillham, where one of the council members lived, and he'd found out that Tali was his mate. It would be confusing for anyone, and Julian's mind was reeling, even a few days later. He had to accept there wasn't much he could do to help the assassins, even though they'd helped him, and it didn't go down well. "Better than some people," he added.

Roark nodded curtly. "You helped us. Thank you. I don't know if Tony and the others would have made it out of the infirmary in one piece if you hadn't been there for them."

Julian looked away. He rubbed the back of his neck, wondering how to take Roark's words. "I didn't do anything anyone else wouldn't have done," he finally said.

"I don't know if that's true, but still. Thank you."

"I guess I'm going to go grab my stuff. I'll be out of your hair soon."

He moved toward the stairs, but Roark caught his arm. "You'll be out of my hair?"

"You have to focus on your family, and I'm not part of it." Not yet, maybe not ever. It depended on Tali, and Julian hadn't had the time to talk to him yet. "I can find a motel or something. I'll let you know if anything happens to me, but you shouldn't worry too much. I'm not your problem. I'll be fine."

The glare Roark aimed at Julian made Julian's step falter. "What do you mean, you're not my problem?"

"I'm not a council assassin."

"So? You worked with us. You helped Tony and the others out of the infirmary. I know that without you, things would have gone badly for them. That means that you are part of the family, no matter what you think. You're not going anywhere, Julian. You're with us now, so you'll be staying either in Gillham or with some of the others, depending on where we find space for everyone. And once we have a new place to stay, you'll be coming with us." He paused. "As long as you want that, too. I won't force you. I know that you're in trouble and that we're not equipped to help you at the moment, but we'll figure it out. You can count on that. You helped us, and we're going to help you."

"You already helped me. You allowed me to stay here. It was more than I deserved after what I did." Julian had followed Roark and his friends to a cabin in the mountains and had slashed their tires. He'd tried to ruin their Halloween party, too, until he'd realized that they were organizing the party for kids in a shelter.

He was an asshole.

He still wasn't sure why he'd turned to Roark and the assassins when he'd been in trouble except for the fact that he knew they could help him. He didn't even know who was after him, and it had been hard to ask the assassins for help, especially Roark. He'd expected to be kicked out, but instead, they'd taken him in. They hadn't even taken much time to think about it.

Julian had never realized how close the assassins were. Now that he did, he was amazed by the fact that they'd allowed him to become part of it. He wasn't family quite yet, but he was somewhat part of it, just like Roark had said.

He cleared his throat. "Thank you. I know it would be much easier for you to ask me to leave."

"We won't abandon you, so stop worrying about it. We never leave anyone behind."

"The people after me could find out where I am and bring trouble to Gillham. I don't want that to happen."

Roark patted Julian's shoulder, almost knocking him on his knees. "Don't worry about that, either. If they look for trouble, they'll find it. But we need to rebuild, and in the meantime, we have to be careful. We were all lucky to be able to make it, and I know we'll find a place for everyone while we get the new warehouse in shape, but that doesn't mean someone won't realize where we are and try to take advantage of it. You'll be staying in Gillham with Rocco and the others who were with you when you shimmered there. Keep an eye on them. Rocco can defend himself, but Tony is still healing, and Tali and Jolyn, well, they're not fighters."

"Will you be there, too?"

"I will, but I'm only one man, and I need to have eyes everywhere, just in case."

Julian nodded. "I'll be your eyes, then." Because there was no way Julian would allow anyone to hurt his mate, whether or not Tali ever wanted him.

ABOUT THE AUTHOR

Catherine is the creator of several series, most of them paranormal, including the Whitedell Pride Series and the Gillham Pack Series. While she graduated in translation, she decided to go the writer's way because it was more fun to create her own stories and characters.

She's been living in Italy for more than twenty years, but she's a daughter of the North—Belgium to be precise—and she misses it so much that she's already planning to move back.

She loves pizza—probably too much—her son, her pets, and of course, books. She sneaks some reading time into her schedule every time she has five minutes free from writing, demands from her various pets and son, and lastly, housework.

Connect with her:
lievens.catherine@gmail.com
BookBub: https://www.bookbub.com/authors/catherine-lievens
Website: https://authorcatherinelievens.com/
Facebook: https://www.facebook.com/catherine.lievens.9
Facebook Group: https://www.facebook.com/groups/411788002341528/
Twitter: https://twitter.com/authorCLievens
Newsletter: http://eepurl.com/c-uvKn

www.ingramcontent.com/pod-product-compliance
Lightning Source LLC
Chambersburg PA
CBHW060637130626
46555CB00002B/842